CLOSURE

An Eli Quinn Detective Novella

Robert Roy Britt

Published by Ink • Spot
P.O. Box 74693
Phoenix, Arizona 85087
InkSpotBooks.com
Published in the United States of America
First printing, 2016

Cover by Trent Design

Closure/Robert Roy Britt. 1st ed.
ISBN 978-0-9977614-1-2

What readers are saying about Closure

"Fascinating plot . . . a great read."

"A great read. Very enjoyable."

"I really enjoyed this book. Quinn is not the usual detective."

— Via Amazon.com

*For Mom, who has always known
there was more to the story.*

CHAPTER 1

I got out of the red Jeep Wrangler pissed at the world. Unlocked the front door of our modest, one-story, three-bed, two-bath. Correction: *my* one-story, three-bed, two-bath.

Solo was just inside the door, his tail slapping the wall, tongue wagging like a counterbalance out front. Every inch of Solo wanted to jump on me, but he waited until I said "Up!" then put his paws on my belt, got a quick pat on the head and a two-handed scratch behind the ears. Solo put his paws back on the floor and was at my side.

I got a Sierra Nevada from the fridge, popped the top, went through the living room, opened the sliding glass doors and went into the back yard. It was in the high eighties, climbing to the mid nineties, a dry and comfortable Arizona spring day.

Sitting on a wrought-iron chair Jess had picked out, half the beer went down in one go. I scratched Solo behind the ears, said "Fuck" too loudly, and wondered what the hell I would do now.

I pulled my iPhone out of its holster, thought about calling the managing editor at *The Arizona Republic*. Nick Zee had been great when Jess was killed, telling me to take off as much time as needed. Days turned to weeks and then months as I chased down her killer. Now with the trial done, and her killer going to jail for a long, long time, I had no clue what was next.

I set the iPhone down on the arm of the chair, not ready to go back to work. Zee had been trying to get me to return for several weeks. "For your own good, Quinn," he said.

But back in the office there'd be the daily routine of reporting on things that used to seem so important but now just felt somehow trivial. Then again, I couldn't just sit around the house. Didn't have anything else in mind.

***

The doorbell rang. Solo jumped to attention and barked the deep, commanding bark of a German shepherd, just once, as was his habit. If it had been a stranger, he'd be growling now. Instead, he stuck his tongue out and made the happy smile dogs do. He knew who was at the door. I didn't know whether it was sounds or smells that told this 110-pound attack dog who was out front, but he always seemed to know. His enthusiastic trot toward the door, with a constant look back that said, "are you not going to run and open this door really quickly?" gave me a good idea who it was.

I walked in through the slider, through the house, and opened the front door.

Sam Marcos pushed past, letting herself in as she sometimes did lately, like a fresh breeze in slim jeans and a light blue t-shirt. She slapped a thigh and Solo raised up on his hind legs and gave her his paws. She nuzzled him, spoke a little girl-to-dog talk that only the two of them could possibly understand. Solo licked her face enthusiastically. Some attack dog.

I'd known Samantha Marcos for years. We worked

several stories together at the paper, respected each other's talents, and had become good friends the past year while I looked for Jess' killer. Sam was full of determination, had a Mediterranean temper and a surprising bravado, all accented perfectly by long, straight black hair, olive skin and dark brown eyes that I had tried hard not to get lost in many times. I usually succeeded. It was never easy.

See, there were two problems.

Before Jess was killed, our marriage had been going downhill. We were trying to fix it, then suddenly she was gone. Violently gone. I was buried under remorse and sadness and guilt. Most of it was still there. The second problem was that Sam and I were easy together, comfortable. With Jess gone, Sam became an even closer friend. She helped me find Jess' killer.

All this was confusing to me. Sometimes I hated myself for even thinking about it. Sometimes I tried to be less judgmental of me, and to explain myself to myself. Mostly I stayed confused.

Whatever, I always felt better when Sam was around than when she wasn't, and sometimes I just had to not think about why. This was a skill I was honing, but very, very slowly.

"I saw the verdict on the wire," Sam said. "Sorry I couldn't be there. Deadlines, you know. Figured you'd be home now."

I closed the door, looked down, pushed a swirl of dog hair around with my shoe.

"So," Sam said. "It's done. I'm glad for you, and I'm sorry. You OK?"

"Don't know if I'll ever be OK. You know that."

"Listen, Quinn. You did everything you could."

"Sam ..."

"Sorry. But ... I just don't want to see you mope around now. It's been a year. I know it still hurts. I know you'll never get over it. That's fine, but ..." She shut her mouth, looked embarrassed. Quieter: "Oh God, Quinn. Are you all right?"

"You don't know a damn thing, Sam." I turned away, shoved my hands into the pockets of my jeans, headed for the fridge.

"I'm sorry," she said. "I'm really sorry that all this happened to you. Sorry I can't understand it the way you do. But we're friends, and you're important to me. I have a job to do now. And my job is to make you get back on your feet, even if you don't want to. It's time." Her voice had become stern.

I opened the fridge, got another beer. "You want one?"

"No, thanks. I don't drink in the middle of the day."

"Me neither." I opened it and took a long pull.

"He was a nutjob," Sam said. "You have to stop blaming yourself."

"That your professional opinion?"

"It is."

I stared off into empty space for a moment. It was hard sometimes to look at Sam Marcos. She always seemed to know where my mind was going. I didn't know how much of it owed to her degree in psychology, how much was simply a connection between the two of us, but it felt like she knew me better even than Jess had. Sam was smart, insightful and tenacious. And her dark eyes could cast a spell. The truth was, Sam stirred feelings I didn't want stirred. The guilt again. I shook my head to try and clear it. It all stayed murky up there.

"We've been through this, Sam."

"He would've killed someone else if it hadn't been …"

I threw the half-full beer bottle at a kitchen cabinet, where it hit with a thud, fell to the granite counter and shattered. I didn't mean to. Sometimes my hands just did things that needed to be done. And doing this didn't feel bad. It was like letting a little steam out of a pressure relief valve so the whole thing wouldn't blow. My face was hot.

My chin quivered slightly.

She stepped back, but didn't freak out. I felt like a steel bar pulled back and ready to fly forward, or snap. My jaw flexed and I heard my teeth grind.

"I'm sorry," Sam said. "I didn't mean to say it like that. I just meant that it's not your fault. That idiot was on a mission, an evil mission, and you know his victim was random."

"The random victim was my wife!" I stared at Sam as though it was her fault. She didn't flinch. It wasn't the first time I'd yelled at her. Not really *at* her, but at life, with her the only one there to take it. She went to the pantry and pulled out the dustpan, started to scoop the broken glass from the counter into it.

"Don't do that," I said.

Sam didn't say anything.

"You don't have to."

"I know," she said.

"Then why do you?"

"I don't know. It's no big deal. Maybe because I know you need some help, even if you won't admit it." She paused. Then quieter: "Maybe because I worry about you being in the proximity of broken glass." The glass clinked as she poured it into the wastebasket.

"That's not something you need to worry about."

"I know. I know. But dammit, Quinn, today has to bring a little closure. You deserve that."

"Why do you care?"

"I care. That's all. I care." Her eyes narrowed. Anger flashed. "It's what friends do," she said. "Jesus, Quinn. I've spent more time with you the past year than anyone. I know you pretty damn well. I think you know me. Maybe all that doesn't mean much to you, but I care."

I sighed. My shoulders slumped. I flexed my fingers to relax my hands. I walked around the breakfast bar and over to the open slider. I put my hands up on the jamb, stared at

5

Pinnacle Peak. I didn't talk for a minute.

Sam waited. Sam was good at waiting.

"I'm sorry," I said. "Thank you for coming over. You know I appreciate it. But I don't know what I'm going to do. I really don't. Finding Jess' killer and waiting to see him convicted kept me busy. It gave me something important to do." My head swiveled slowly side-to-side. "Now I don't know. I don't know."

Sam let me stand there with my thoughts a moment.

"Listen, I came for a reason," she finally said.

"Oh, good. Not just to see my smiling face?"

I turned toward her and tried to smile, but I just didn't have it in me.

"You won't go back, will you?"

"To the paper?"

"Yeah," she said.

"I don't see how. It used to be fun. I loved the challenge. I did good things. *We* did good things. Now the place will just be a constant reminder of everything that went wrong. And what good did I do, really? Ferreting out corporate greed and political malfeasance when there are killers on the loose."

"You don't *have* to go back."

She was right. My savings and investments would carry me for a good long time.

"No, I don't have to work. At least not for a few years. I can just drink and enjoy the sun."

"Quinn, I know you better than that. You need something to do, some purpose."

"What the hell is worth doing? I can continue to investigate small-time crime in Arizona business and politics, rat out the sheriff for backward, discriminatory policies that Arizona voters don't care about, report on the Corporation Commission's cozy relationship with the power company ..." I slumped into the leather club chair, put my head in my hands, and finally the tears came. I'd held them off for a year, told myself I couldn't afford any more of them after the funeral.

Sam waited until I was done. It took a while. But it felt like I'd gotten rid of something. I couldn't say what, but something that had rotted inside me felt flushed out. I leaned back, rested my head on the back of the chair. Eyes closed. Arms on the chair arms, fingers gripping.

"You have to do something," she said again.

"Like?"

"Detective."

I tipped my head forward slightly, closed my eyes even tighter. "What?"

"Detective." She spoke quickly. "You know. Private investigator. Amateur detective. Whatever. You're good at it. You have the mind for it. You have the drive for it. Once you start to zero in on a problem, nothing stops you. You know how you did it as a reporter, poking this way and that, circling closer and closer until the truth is flushed out like a pheasant. And there will always be people who need help. You don't need a lot of income, so you can pick and choose your cases, do *good* things."

I opened my eyes, then narrowed them.

"I don't know the first thing about being a detective. Finding Jess' killer was something I couldn't *not* do."

"You'll learn. Meanwhile, you're smart, you're inquisitive, and you're like a fucking bloodhound once you get on a trail."

"Where did this idea come from?"

"Delores Bernstein needs someone like you."

"Who?"

"Delores Bernstein. The woman whose husband was killed last week up in country club, three nights after they'd been broken into and had a computer stolen."

"Oh, yeah, I read your story. They haven't found the guy."

"Nope. Sheriff Otto is saying it was maybe a random

break-in attempt by a druggie or an illegal." She affected a sheriff-like deep voice: "Arizona is a dangerous place and Tinker Bernstein was home alone at the wrong time."

"But?"

"The case is too weird. First off, there's never been a shooting in country club. Ten years. And there've been only a handful of burglaries."

"Because it's gated," I said.

"Right. Now the Bernsteins suffer both in a three-day span? The wife, Delores, doesn't have an alibi, so the sheriff still suspects her. But I've gotten to know her, and I think this whole thing is killing her. A random murder. Life seems pointless. Delores loved her husband—married thirty years, and from what I knew they were as in love as ever. Now she's alone in a big empty house and she's scared. She needs somebody to give her some hope. Help her find closure. I figure that's something you know a thing or two about."

"Sounds more like a job for a therapist."

"Delores thinks it was more than just a break-in gone bad," Sam said. "And she insists she didn't do it. She needs somebody to dig deeper than the sheriff's office seems willing to do."

"What do you think?"

"Apparently he was killed in his chair in his garage-turned-office. Delores thinks the garage door might have been open at the time. And she feels like they knew he'd be there, and they knew she wasn't there."

I looked at random things around the room, not registering them. It's what I do sometimes when I'm thinking, kind of block out sight and sound, focus all energy on thought. I don't even think about it. Thinking, that is. I asked, "These people are rich, yes?"

"Very."

"As in?"

"Enough to buy a million-dollar home, furnish it to the nines, expensive art, neither of them work."

"And let me guess, he had an expensive life insurance policy."

"Naturally. Three million. But Delores insists she doesn't need that money. They don't appear to have any significant debts."

"Money is a great motivator," I said. "She could have been into some sort of trouble he didn't know about."

"I know. But if you meet her, get to know her, listen to the facts, I don't know. I think you'll agree with me that this thing stinks. There's something more going on."

"Not the greatest security up there," I said.

"But enough that when people want to break into a house, they usually find one outside the gates."

"Like mine."

"Like yours."

"I've never been broken into," I said.

"Not a lot of crime in Pleasant."

Pleasant. I know. But that's the name of our town. They have some weird town names in Arizona. Tombstone, Hog Eye, and even one called Why. Pleasant? Why not.

I said, "But two crime scenes in three days up in the country club, and both at the same house."

"And none of the art was taken. I didn't write that in my article, because here's this woman living alone with I assume seven figures worth of art on the wall. It didn't feel right to expose that vulnerability."

I thought about all that. Sam let me think. What I figured out was that she had planted the seed she came to plant. It was an interesting seed, I had to admit.

"Private investigator," I said. "I don't know the rules. Probably supposed to pack a gun. You know I don't like guns. I'd also have to keep a pint of bourbon or something in my right-hand desk drawer, right? I don't drink bourbon."

"You could try wine."

"Wine in a drawer sounds like a serious drinking

problem."

My face softened a little. Not quite a smile, but I managed an audible *humph* to acknowledge something beyond the darkness I'd been wrapped in. My body relaxed slightly. My brain kept turning things over on its own, circling around the central issue of what to do with the rest of my life. I could feel the thoughts spiraling together, like matter pulled to a center of gravity. It didn't take long for the decision to become obvious, then inevitable.

"I suppose that means they'll call me a ... nevermind."

"A dick? Not sure they use that term much anymore. But I can call you one if you want. Accurate as often as not."

I grinned. Something I hadn't done much lately. "I'd rather you don't."

"I'll take the beer now," she said.

CHAPTER 2

Choi's Martial Arts was located on the southwest side of Pleasant's town center, in the older, less expensive part of the gridded streets, south of Tranquil Trail and a block west of Pleasant Way. An auto-repair shop on one side, a small nursery selling native plants on the other. The multicolored adobe façade gave way to a simple, large industrial space with a stained concrete floor and a central sparring mat of interconnecting squares of red and blue.

I bowed slightly as I entered the building. Removed my shoes and put them in a cubby. Bowed deeply before walking onto the mat. I'd changed at home into the simple white uniform with black trim, black belt with four gold stripes.

It was early afternoon on a Monday, the dojo empty. Master Choi, at five-foot-five and in his mid-fifties, was probably in his office doing paperwork or napping. He napped a lot, and when he wasn't napping, he could go from the fully seated position to knocking an apple off the top of the head of a six-foot man with a kick that didn't muss the man's hair, all in the space of a second.

I sat in the center of the mat and stretched. Could almost

do the splits, but had never quite achieved it fully. It was about trying, and so I kept trying but not succeeding. I warmed up with some air punches and kicks, a few jumping jacks, some jump squats. Sprinted from one side of the mat to the other, walked back, and repeated that twenty times. Kicked the bag. Ten roundhouse kicks with each leg, in rapid succession without my kicking foot touching the ground, then a series of side kicks with each leg, back kicks, back spinning hook kicks. Rest thirty seconds. Repeat. After twenty minutes I'd worked up a good sweat and forgotten about the outside world. All focus was on the bag. Me and the bag.

I went to the back room, a cramped space with a full set of free weights. I preferred it to a regular gym. No distracting spandex. No music, no muscle heads showing off, and nobody socializing. Just me and the weights. I did fifteen reps each on a circuit, cycling through the bench, curls, overhead presses, flies front and back, then squats. Old school. No DVD or app required. I repeated the cycle three times. The whole workout took less than fifteen minutes. I was breathing heavily.

I did the same weight workout three times a week. It kept me strong and gave me endurance. Combined with the running, it made me feel as though I could outrun, or outlast, just about any foe. I didn't have many foes, but it was a good feeling in case one came along.

Back in the dojo, I worked through my latest form, the one I'd need to master before I could test for fifth degree. It was harder to do forms after a heavy workout, and that was the point.

I didn't see or hear Master Choi step onto the mat and come up behind me. Almost the instant I saw him out of the corner of my eye, I felt and heard the thwack on my arm of the bamboo stick he used to correct positions of arms and legs, hands and feet, sometimes even a chin or forehead. It was loud, and it hurt, a pain I'd gotten used to a long time ago.

"Lower." Then another, lighter tap with the stick. "Lower. There."

There were two ways to do forms, called poomsae: The right way, and the wrong way. Master Choi didn't tolerate the wrong way, and it didn't matter if you were an orange belt or a fourth-degree black belt, he would whack you when you got it wrong.

"All up here," Master Choi said, pointing at his temple. "Focus!"

For the next half hour, I went through all my forms, in reverse order, down to and including the white belt form I'd learned from a different master, in New York, when I was twelve. Master Choi had forced me to relearn them all when I came to his dojo a few years ago as a third-degree black belt. The changes were subtle, the new positions far superior.

After working with me a year and, best I could tell, trusting my character, he had shown me several additional ways to disarm or kill a man. "Never use, if not need," he said at the end of every deadly lesson, always held privately. The sessions further built my confidence and respect for the devastation my hands and feet could inflict, if needed.

After forms, Master Choi made me do some of the most basic kicks, twenty with each foot. It was white-belt stuff, but I didn't complain. It was part of the taekwondo philosophy: learn, repeat, repeat, repeat. And when you have it mastered, repeat it some more, and then again.

I finished twenty basic front snap kicks with my left foot, starting each time with the right foot forward. It was the first kick I'd learned, nearly two decades ago. I was getting really fucking tired, and the last two were poorly done.

"Again," Master Choi said.

I willed the exhaustion into a mental box and did twenty more with my left foot, all expertly, if I do say so.

"Sushi fee," Master Choi said sharply.

His command of English was somewhat less than his martial arts skills. I switched my feet, put the left one forward, and executed twenty textbook front snap kicks with my right foot.

We bowed to the American and Korean flags on the wall. I was fully spent. But for ninety minutes, I hadn't thought about Jess, Sam, Delores Bernstein, or anything else.

CHAPTER 3

The red Jeep's top was down, the temperature perfect. Sam Marcos was in the passenger seat, Solo in back, smiling with his head sticking out the side and the wind flapping his jowls at forty miles an hour as we headed up Pleasant Way, toward the suburban part of town around the base of Pinnacle Peak.

Pleasant was an eclectic mishmash, an Old West town center with apartments above shops in a grid surrounded by meandering suburban streets and adobe-style homes. Wealthy newcomers lived among real cowboys and working-class families that went back generations.

The deejay on KJZZ with the Barry White voice said the temperature was seventy-four, heading to a high of ninety-five. If life hadn't sucked so much the past year, I might've enjoyed it.

I turned left into the country club and stopped at the gatehouse. The country club was much like the rest of Pleasant's, except home prices were higher and access to the private golf course was possible if you paid a big fee.

The guard was balding and sweaty, a sloppy-looking man with a lifetime of drinking and disappointment creased into his doughy face. He worked for a private security company contracted to keep unwanted people out of the country club.

The pink-faced man was not menacing. He didn't look like he would win any fights, but the way he approached slowly, on his time, the way he pulled his trousers up and puffed his chest out, the way he smirked as though it we'd be privileged to enter, suggested this was *his* gate, and nobody was getting through unless he said so. Solo didn't move a muscle below the neck, didn't growl, didn't give any indication of the aggression he could pour on faster than I could say "attack," but he never took his eyes off the gatemaster.

"How can I help you?" the rotund man asked in a voice higher than expected. He looked right past me and eyed Sam. Sweat beaded on his forehead. Nametag on his shirt said "Johnson" under a Dribbs Security label.

Sam leaned forward. "Visiting Delores Bernstein. I'm Sam Marcos."

I watched the gatemaster's eyes flick down to Sam's chest and back up again quickly.

"Oh, yes, hi Ms. Marcos. I remember you from before. They find the killer yet?"

"Nope. Still looking."

"Terrible thing. Terrible. Listen. Tinker Bernstein was a nice guy. Didn't talk much, but a nice guy."

Johnson looked down, shook his head and pulled his trousers up over a lifetime of snacks. He ogled Sam again, didn't have anything else to say, glanced briefly at me as if noticing me for the first time, then back at Sam, and smiled. Finally, he cleared his throat and found some words.

"Listen, ah, I have to call Mrs. Bernstein before I can let you in. New rules. You understand."

"Of course," Sam said.

Johnson waddled back to the gatehouse, picked up a conventional telephone, punched some numbers.

"New rules," I said to Sam.

"Yeah, no surprise. Used to be pretty lax. I could get in just because the guards knew who I was—the ones who knew me never asked where I was going. Even when a new guard would come in, I'd just tell him where I was going, and he'd buzz me through."

"Probably your sexy outfit."

"Yeah, you know me. Miss Arizona. And my secret weapon: I'm naked underneath all this."

I looked straight ahead, not a twitch. Refocused on my new job. *Eli Quinn, Private Detective.*

Johnson hung up, angled to the rear of the Jeep and apparently jotted down my license plate number, even though they photographed it with a camera mounted on the overhang of the shack. He made his way back to the driver's door.

"You Eli Quinn?"

"Yes, sir." I had never used the salutation so loosely.

"Friend of Ms. Marcos?"

Johnson had lowered his voice, pulled his chin in, hiked his trousers again. I didn't like the glint in his eye. Half wanted to punch him. Half didn't, for logical reasons related to the jail time or lawsuit that might result. I held the steering wheel tightly with both hands and held my tongue.

"Mr. Quinn?"

"We're friends, yes."

Johnson smiled. I gripped the steering wheel harder. Sam leaned back, cleared her throat in a manner that suggested, *easy, Quinn.* Solo let loose the absolute smallest of growls, so deep and subtle that Johnson didn't appear to hear it.

"Mrs. Bernstein said you'd be with Ms. Marcos. You can go right in. But listen. Make sure you keep that dog on a leash. Looks friendly and all, but that's the rules."

"Will do," I said cheerily, with no intention of putting Solo on a leash.

Johnson pushed a button and the gate arm lifted up.

"Have a nice day," he said as we drove ahead.

When we passed out of earshot, I said: "Interesting they write down your license plate, even though they photograph it."

"Yes. Foolproof system, I'm sure."

"Mmm-hmm."

We wound through the lazy streets of the country club.

"Left here," Sam said, pointing at the next stop sign.

The farther in you went, the emptier the streets became. Like capillaries off an artery, the streets served fewer and fewer cells. I turned onto Wolf Pack Way, wondering why anyone would name a street that, in a place with abundant coyotes and no wolves for hundreds of miles.

"You're quiet," Sam said.

"Just thinking."

"About?"

"Absolutely nothing."

"I don't believe in that possibility."

"Yeah, well, I mean, nothing worth mentioning. Sometimes my mind just drifts off into meaningless thoughts. It's one way to stop thinking about bad things and let my brain rest."

"You're a complex man, Eli Quinn."

She motioned another left turn, and I took it.

"Wife was a suspect at one point, right?"

"Spouse is often suspected until ruled out," Sam said.

"Us detectives know that, of course."

"Then why'd you ask, dick?"

"I make it my business to ask questions, not make assumptions."

"Smart. Clearly you've been at this a while."

"Seventeen minutes, to be precise. And that's if you count the time it took me to swing by and pick you up."

"Sheriff still hasn't ruled her out," Sam said. "She—Delores—says she wasn't home when her husband was killed. She went out to buy a gift for one of her grandkids.

When she came home, she took the long way around through the country club to watch the sunset, otherwise she would have been home a few minutes earlier. She says she came home, went in and took a shower. It was a while before she found her husband, and some more time before she called 9-1-1. When the police arrived, she was covered in blood."

"She was in shock, went to him, held him, panicked, all that."

"Right," Sam said. "They never found any motive or any other evidence to suggest she did it. I think it's silly they considered her a suspect."

"Except for the clock on the wall."

"Except that."

"Stopped at 6:59."

"Bullet straight through the center of it," Sam said.

"Why?"

"Nobody knows," she said.

"You think she did it?"

"Her story sounds a little screwy, but she tells it convincingly. And she just doesn't seem like a killer."

"They often don't."

CHAPTER 4

Solo stayed in the Jeep, under the shade of the mesquite tree. Sam pushed a the doorbell. Delores Bernstein opened the front door. She looked late fifties, had already cut her hair short and curled it, the way older women do. Her faced was wrinkled, and despite wearing makeup well, she looked tired and older than she was.

"Hi Delores," Sam said. "This is Eli Quinn." She tilted her head my way.

"Please, come in," the woman said, her voice throaty but crackling slightly like the mother on *Everybody Loves Raymond*—again, sounding older than she was. She pulled the door open and backed out of the way. She didn't look like a killer. But you never knew. Neighbors were always saying, "I can't believe he would do such a thing!" Less frequently were they asked if *she* would do such a thing. No one ever suspects a woman.

"Hello Mrs. Bernstein," I said, nodding with a slight bow, keeping my eyes up just in case she pulled a knife or a gun on me or something.

"Please. Delores."

"Yes ma'am."

She wore a black kimono-sleeve sweater over a long-sleeve white cotton t-shirt, black slacks, expensive-looking leather sandals.

"Can I get you something? Coffee? Water? Scotch?"

We both declined politely and were led through the entryway into a grand living room, with nine-foot ceilings, white marble floors, walls painted in the rich colors of the Southwest, expensive, stuffy loud-print-fabric furniture. The gold and green drapes were pulled open to reveal a giant wall of windows opening onto a well manicured backyard that dropped off into a shallow wash, leaving nothing but sky and a perfectly framed Pinnacle Peak. The walls showcased paintings I assumed were not purchased at the mall.

The house was cold, air conditioning no doubt running up a big bill. Sam and I sat on the sofa, close enough that our thighs touched. I didn't need that distraction. I moved over a few inches. Delores sat on an overstuffed Queen Ann facing us.

"Quinn is interested in looking for your husband's killer," Sam said.

"I'm sorry for your loss," Delores said.

I was confused for a moment. I looked at Sam, then back at Mrs. Bernstein. Then realized what she meant.

"Oh, yes. Well, it's been a year," was all I could come up with.

"You tracked down the killer."

"Yes."

"Can you find my husband's killer?"

"I don't know. But I think I'd like to try."

"Why?"

I wasn't sure how to answer that. This woman had recently lost her husband. Assuming she wasn't the murderer, she was probably desperate for answers. Like me. The whole time I wondered about Jess' murderer and worked to find him. Like me, Delores Bernstein probably wasn't in the mood to be bullshitted.

"I need something to do," I said. "I think I can be good at this."

"What do you charge?"

I hadn't considered that. But I suddenly realized I'd already known the answer. I wasn't rich, but I'd made good money on Wall Street in my twenties. I tired of finance, but I'd invested wisely in a few hot tech stocks, and sold most of my shares before the market decline. It wasn't brilliance, just luck and prudence. I put the money into treasuries and dividend-paying blue chips. I went back to school and got a journalism degree, landed a job at the *Pleasant Weekly Herald* — the only offer I got as a 30-year-old graduate from an obscure journalism program—and a year later was picked off by *The Arizona Republic*, where after just a couple years I was promoted to senior writer and put on investigative projects. The pay was lousy, but I didn't need much, and the work was far more rewarding. I still had most of my investments intact. The dividends covered a modest living, and that's all I really wanted.

"There's no charge, Mrs. Bernstein. This isn't about money. I know how you feel, and I want to help." If she was the killer, I was already the worst detective in Arizona, feeling her pain, empathizing, volunteering to help.

"I'd feel better if I paid you something. I'm not a charity case. I need to know you're serious."

My gut told me she was indeed grieving, but I was just as sure she was a rock, always had been. I decided to keep an open mind on whether or not she might've killed her husband.

"Unfortunately, I'm always serious," I said.

"Is that some sort of joke, Mr. Quinn?"

"Not at all. I just mean that my life hasn't been a barrel of laughs the past year, and I may have lost some of the humor and lightness I once had. But my whole life, when there's something needs doing, I've been serious about getting it done." I paused, looked at the floor, realized I was leaning forward, shoulders tensed, my whole body tight. I shouldn't be trying to sell myself so hard. It sounded like insecurity. I relaxed my shoulders consciously, took a deep breath and let it out slowly, forced my emotions back down to where they'd come from.

"When I put my mind to something, I'm very serious about it," I said. "I want to do this, and I'll give it my best. Paying me would just be awkward. I don't need the money right now. And since I'm not officially a detective, it wouldn't seem appropriate." Maybe not even legal. I looked at my first potential client, realized I'd given a lousy sales pitch. She stared at me, her head cocked back slightly. Chin jutted out. Eyes narrowed a bit. I wasn't sure which way the decision would go.

"If the killer can be found, Mrs. Bernstein, I'll find him. There's nothing else I need to do right now. I would focus exclusively on this."

Delores held my gaze. Her mouth was shut tight. I thought I saw her chin quiver slightly. If acting, she was good. I knew the emotion behind that quiver, had felt it many times in the past year. It could come at any moment, unannounced, unexpected, unrelated to the moment. She tilted her head forward slightly, smoothed her slacks on her thighs.

"Thank you, Sam. I like this man Eli Quinn."

"As do I," Sam said.

I looked at the floor again.

"Let me get us some coffee," Delores said.

***

As Sam and I waited for Delores to return with coffee neither of us wanted, we looked around the living room.

I asked in a low voice, "How much you think all these paintings are worth?"

"A lot, I suppose," Sam whispered.

There were three sculptures in the room. One appeared to be two women having sex, but no matter how I looked at it, I couldn't tell which limb belonged to which woman. Another was a bust of someone probably famous, but I didn't know who. The other was a bust of Ben Franklin. Ben, his head and part of his shoulders perched atop a narrow pedestal, looked wise but wistful, lazy lids covering eyes that gazed off to one side and down, thin lips pulled back as if tired from all the work that went into founding a country.

On the coffee table in front of the sofa were copies of *National Geographic, Martha Stewart Living, Scientific American, House Beautiful, Popular Mechanics* and *Make* magazine. I thumbed through a copy of *Make*, the modern do-it-yourselfer's bible. How to build an underwater robot. How to make your own Geiger counter. Devise a rear-view power socket. Make a gin pole, whatever that was.

Delores returned from the kitchen with three white ceramic cups of coffee on a tray. "Please, help yourself," she said.

Sam declined. I didn't want any either, but I took one of the cups, sipped the coffee black. "Thank you," I said.

"Now what do you need to know about my husband?"

"Tell me a little about what he did, how he came to be retired," I said.

"Tinker was an engineer at heart, built computer systems that controlled airplane systems. He ended up being a vice president at GE, overseeing a bunch of other engineers. GE paid him well, good pension, and he inherited quite a bit of money when his parents died."

Her voice was flat. Sounded rehearsed. But she'd probably had to tell the story more than once in the past few days, and she'd be bored with it. Or maybe the only way to recite the story without tears was to do it in monotone and try consciously to avoid emotion. "Over the years he started collecting art, just as a hobby at first. He was good at it, and he made money on the few pieces he sold. He retired two years ago and other than buying and selling art, he spends ... spent ... most of his time making things. She looked down. Her eyes watered. I waited. She sniffed a bit, and looked up again.

"I'm sorry, ma'am."

"Please, call me Delores."

"Yes ma'am." I wasn't sure what level of formality to strike with my first client, who was also a murder suspect, at least technically. I'd have to look that one up in the private investigator manual. "Was your husband, Mr. Bernstein, was he handy around the house?"

"Oh, yes," she said. "Tinker could fix anything. If something wasn't broken, he'd tear it apart anyway, just to figure out how it worked. Or he'd make it better. He built his own computer. I never understood most of it."

"You told me the other day," Sam said, "That's where the nickname came from."

"Of course," Delores said, repeating the story for me. "He got the nickname as a kid, and it fit perfectly. He is, was, more than anything else, a tinkerer. When we met, I tried to call him Caleb, but he insisted I call him Tinker. He said he never liked the way his first name ended with the same sound as his last name began. Caleb Bernstein was hard to pronounce, he said, and when he had to use it for official things, he always had to spell it. Nobody had trouble spelling Tinker."

"So Mr. Bernstein was out in his office when he ..." I let the sentence tail off. My approach to asking detective questions wasn't well developed yet.

"When he was killed," Delores finished for me. "It's OK, Mr. Quinn. You can say it. I still can't believe it, but I don't want to pretend it didn't happen. Yes, he—Tinker—was out in the garage. We have two. When we bought the place, he converted one to a workshop. Much more than an office, but he has his office desk out there, too."

"Doesn't it get a little hot in the summer?"

"He put in a separate air conditioner, insulated the walls. Did most of the work himself. He loved it out there."

"So Mr. Bernstein was out there, in the garage."

"Tinker, please. Call him Tinker."

"Yes ma'am," I said. "Just before seven p.m., correct?"

"That's what the sheriff says, yes."

"How did the killer, or killers, get in?"

"The deputies figure they simply walked in," she said. "I left to go to the Desert Ridge mall at around 5:30. The main garage door was open when I left. It was a warm evening. We don't get much traffic up here—only neighbors. We're at the end of the street."

"And you said you returned a little after seven."

"Yes. I would've been home sooner." She paused to emphasize the importance of the timing. "But when I came through the gate, I saw the sun was about to set. There were a few clouds to the west, and they were turning red, so I took the long way around, on Pinnacle Drive. When you get up to the highest point, there's a clear view of Pinnacle Peak in one direction, and the sunset in the other. Tinker and I went there often to watch the sunset. I knew there wasn't time to stop and pick him up, so I went there, stopped for a few minutes, and watched the sun go down. It was beautiful."

"And when you returned, was the garage door open?"

"No, it was closed. I parked in the driveway—we don't have a lot of garage space—went in the front door, hollered for him and didn't hear anything but some piano concerto. But that was normal. Tinker usually played classical when he was working. I took a shower, started dinner, and then wondered why he hadn't come in. I found him around eight o'clock." Her voice cracked and faltered, but she remained sitting erect, her hands in her lap.

"And when you were broken into three days earlier, how

did they get in?"

"Also through the garage," she said. "But they broke in through the garage side door."

"And you were both away, right?"

"Yes, we'd gone to a fundraiser at the MIM down in Scottsdale."

The Musical Instrument Museum, a short drive from Pleasant, brought in some amazing performers in classical, jazz, rock, folk, blues and sundry other genres for intimate performances. Jess and I had attended several in our the first years together, before the relationship started to strain and we were more apt to spend evenings at home watching TV, working—or pretending to work.

I asked, "They didn't set off your home alarm?"

"He had never set the alarm up in the garage," she said.

"You passed through the guard gate on the way out to the fundraiser that evening," I said.

"Yes, of course," she said. "Why do you ask?"

"I guess that's my new job, Mrs. Bernstein. I'm supposed to ask a lot of questions, then see if the answers add up to anything. Can you show me the garage?"

We went through the kitchen and into the garage. It still had a bare concrete floor and a big garage door. The door was covered in aftermarket insulation. Along the back wall were cabinets over a long workbench with a drill press, a small band saw, and various power tools scattered around.

In the middle of the garage was a large office desk. I recognized the high-end 3D printer, a commercial-grade model that probably cost north of $200,000, and the separate 3D scanner, also not cheap. There was a keyboard, a mouse and two inexpensive flat-screen monitors, but where there would have been a computer under the desk, there wasn't.

"Did your husband still do any work for GE or any other companies, or was he fully retired?

"He quit cold turkey. Fully embraced retirement."

"You said he built his own computer. Was it something particularly valuable?"

"I don't know," she said. "But I think it was a bit of a dinosaur. It looked like something out of the eighties. A big, unattractive box with lots of things connected to it."

"Mac or PC?"

"PC, I guess."

"They stole the PC," I said, "but none of the peripherals."

"Yes, whoever broke in the first time took the computer, and the TV." She pointed to a bare spot on the wall where a TV mount had been ripped off.

Next to the desk chair there was a large bloodstain on the concrete. Otherwise the garage looked like any tinkerer's space, or rather any really *rich* tinkerer's space. *Maker*, I corrected myself. That's what the tinkerers called themselves these days.

"They didn't take anything else?"

"No," she said.

"No cash, no other valuables, none of the art on the walls?"

"Nothing we noticed," she said. "They didn't even come into the house, though we always left the door between the garage and the house unlocked. That door is alarmed though, so the alarm company would've known if they'd gone into the house, and we would have gotten a call on Tinker's cell phone."

"And when they—or whoever—came three nights later and, ah, well, did they take anything?"

"I'm pretty sure they took some tools from the garage. He had a cordless drill that I'd given him for his birthday, and I can't find it now. There's a toolbox missing. It was red and always sat in the same place, and it's gone. Maybe some other things, but as you can see," she waved her arm in a semicircle to indicate the workbench in the back of the garage, "there's still a lot of stuff here."

"His wallet, maybe?"

"No."

"And somebody shot the clock." I pointed at the clock, but looked at her. She nodded. "At 6:59," I said. I couldn't think of anything else to say about that, so I didn't. But it felt like a clue the way a heavy thunderstorm feels like rain. Then again, as a reporter I hadn't spent a lot of time piecing together murder scenes. I didn't feel like a real detective yet. But I was asking a lot of questions and trying to be observant. I was good at observing and had a good memory for details, so I let my mind absorb what I saw and heard, and figured it would get around to putting things together later.

We went back into the house.

"After the break-in, did your husband say anything about what was on the PC? Maybe a valuable file of some sort?"

"No."

"Did he seem nervous about anything?"

"No. I mean, we were shaken up—it's the first time we've ever been broken into. But I don't think he was any more nervous than I was, no."

"And did they enter the house the night they killed him?"

"I don't know. Since Tinker was home, the alarm wasn't on. But I can't find anything missing in the house."

"Sometimes it's hard to know something is missing until you go looking for it," I said.

"So maybe they came in," Delores said, "but if so, they didn't take anything that I have missed yet."

I looked around at all the art. It was all still hanging on the walls or sitting on pedestals, same as a few minutes ago.

I asked, "Did your husband have any enemies? Any debts? Anyone you might be suspicious of?"

"Heavens no. Tinker was well-liked by the few people who knew him well. Ever since we'd moved to Arizona, he spent most of his time here, at the house. His art dealings were done mostly on the phone or by email. He's always been kind of a recluse, and since we didn't know anyone when we moved here, he just dove into his projects, out in the garage. He could work for hours. The only other thing he threw himself into was golf, mostly with our neighbor Charlie Entwill."

"I may want to talk to Charlie," I said.

"Of course. You can go knock on his door, or I can give you his phone number." She gave me the number. I asked about other close friends, and she told me about them, said they'd all be willing to talk to me.

"Any casual acquaintances who might've known about the art collection?"

She thought a moment. "I doubt it. I mean, he was friendly with people he met—the checkout clerks at Frye's, Jeanine, the nice single mother who cuts his hair over at the barber shop, the guards at the gate. He tended to make small talk with people around here more than he used to. He'd never admit it, but I think he got a little lonely with just me and his projects up here in this gated community. But small talk with people he barely knew seemed to be all the social interaction he needed beyond golf and the occasional function I dragged him to." She looked around the room. "Oh, I suppose, some of the causes we donated too—some of the people who ran them would've known we had some art."

"That's a pretty wide net," I said. Delores nodded. I pondered.

"I hate to ask this," I said, "but I've read about more than a few murders over the years, and most were about drugs, money, love or revenge—often revenge mixed with one of the others. I assume Tinker wasn't into drugs. Money could be involved, but you haven't told me anything that takes me very far down that path yet. But I have to ask: He had a big insurance policy…"

"I don't need the money. *We* didn't need the money. I explained all that to the sheriff. This isn't about the insurance policy."

"Is there any chance Tinker was involved with someone else?"

Rather than flinching, she seemed to relax. Her shoulders dropped, and she gave a feeble smile. "If so, I'd be very surprised," she said. "I suppose no wife would want to believe her husband is cheating on her. But, I mean, I don't think Tinker would be considered handsome by most people. His beauty came mostly from the inside, and I don't think very many people saw it. Tinker and I have been together since college. I loved him, and he loved me." She said it with conviction. "I just don't see him out gallivanting. I mean, we were rarely apart except when he played golf. And anyway, there was no, ah, nothing missing from our, well, let's just say things between us were quite good, despite what you kids might think about people our age."

"I understand," I said. "Sorry to have asked. So, frankly, I'm not sure there's much here to work with, but I think I'd like to go and digest it all. Do you have any theories?"

"No. I can't explain it," Delores said. "Neither can the sheriff. But I can't accept that this was a random act of violence. It might not feel any better to know there was a reason, but I desperately want to know the reason."

"I guess that's why I'm here."

"That's why you're here," Sam said.

At the front door, Delores reached for her purse, on a decorative table that didn't seem to serve any purpose other than being a purse-holder. She pulled out a checkbook. "I'd like to pay you something now. Make this official. What would be an appropriate advance?"

She was persistent, that's for sure. I said, "I tell you what. Let's see how I do. If I solve this, you can pay me something when it's all over. If I don't, I really wouldn't feel right about taking your money."

"So again," she said, "what's your fee?"

Even though I'd already decided I didn't want Mrs.

31

Bernstein's money, I tried to imagine attaching a fee to finding a murderer, to giving closure to a grieving widow. A thousand dollars? Ten thousand? A hundred dollars an hour? Plus expenses? That would mean paperwork. I hated paperwork. But I had my first client now, and she wanted there to be a transaction, maybe just to legitimize the relationship. Perhaps it was an issue of trust, of not feeling like a charity case.

"How about a dollar?" I said.

"A dollar?" Delores Bernstein laughed. It was a brief outburst, from deep inside, as though it'd been suppressed by recent events. I knew that feeling. She sounded and looked younger and more vibrant when she laughed. I felt good for giving her that. I was coming to like Delores Bernstein. I would have to look up the appropriateness of that feeling in my detective manual.

She put the checkbook back in her purse, extended her hand. I shook it. So did Sam. "Thank you, both of you," she said. "I hope you find out who did this."

CHAPTER 5

I had almost nothing to go on in my first case as a detective. And no thoughts came to me just now. So I ran. I kept a slow, steady pace up the hill, listened to my breathing, paid attention to my body, found a rhythm.

The rocky trail lead up one of the lesser known routes just south of Pinnacle Peak up a small but steep and rocky razorback mountain, all a quarter mile from home. A roadrunner darted across the trail. Saguaros dominated the landscape. Ocotillos sprung improbably here and there, sometimes alone, sometimes in clumps of three or four, each splaying up and out like a fountain, or Keith Richards' hair. The ground was firm but rocky. I concentrated on my footing.

It was in the mid-nineties, and within a half mile I had a good sweat going. As the blood flowed, my mind began to work on its own. Facts and assumptions popped into my head unprompted.

Delores Bernstein didn't kill her husband. I didn't think. Can't rule that out. Hiring a private detective with no experience might be a smart diversion. If she didn't do it, she wants me to exonerate her and provide closure on the ugliest chapter in her life. If she did it, and she's confident she can't be caught, hiring me makes her look innocent, maybe discourages the sheriff from looking into it further. Assume she didn't for now. Odds at seventy-thirty.

They were broken into. The thieves took only a TV and a computer from the garage of a house full of art. They didn't break into the house. Probably not the work of anyone who knew them well, who knew Tinker Bernstein was an art collector. Or maybe they knew enough to know there was something of value to steal without setting off an alarm. Yet they left a really expensive 3D printer and scanner. Common thieves wouldn't have known the value of those. And they were heavy—not the sort of thing you imagine a thief carrying under his arm as he runs from a crime scene.

My mind logged the presence of a large, loose rock several paces ahead and somehow knew it would be navigated by the right foot. A few steps later my right foot obeyed.

Three days later someone walked into Tinker Bernstein's garage, which may have been wide open, and shot him. For some reason, the clock is also shot, stops dead at 6:59 p.m. Apparently nothing is stolen other than a few tools and a toolbox. That makes no sense. The alarm wasn't set, so whoever it was might've entered the house. If so, it's not clear what they might've done inside the house, but Delores isn't aware of anything being stolen. She says.

Only close friends and a few people in the art community knew Tinker was an art dealer. If the killing wasn't about love, power or revenge, it was probably about money. All those valuables sitting there, and two crimes in three days. Eight percent chance it's about money. I was missing something important.

My breaths had become gasps, my arms were working hard but had lost their form. I concentrated for a moment on the breathing, made it more efficient, pulled my elbows in. Then I let my thoughts drift again.

Whoever it was, they conveniently killed Tinker while Delores was out for a drive. Did the killer know she was out? Was he parked down the street watching the house? If so, a neighbor might've seen the strange car. People in Pleasant made a point of noticing strange cars, which stood out since just about everyone parked in their garages most of the time. And anyone who came in or out of the country club, there'd be a record of them at the gate.

Without thinking about it, I'd stopped running. My hands were on my hips, eyes staring at nothing in the distance. Breathing heavy but even.

I looked left, northward, and took in a scene I'd enjoyed a hundred times. The ground rose gradually into the base of Pinnacle Peak, which shot up abruptly and was capped by a cluster of bare rocks huddled together and pointing skyward. Around to the southeast was a long range of taller peaks that formed the east border of the Valley. Below and to the south, the horizon raced away, a steady drop in altitude down to the Valley floor. Scottsdale and the rest of the Metro area was enveloped in a slight, low-lying haze.

My mind was putting some facts together in meaningful ways, I hoped. So I resumed running and let it continue.

The fact that Delores Bernstein was out for an hour, precisely when her husband was killed, three days after a break-in, was too coincidental to be a coincidence. Not exactly a clue, but at least a lead. And there was something else: Dribbs Security, the outfit that ran security for the country club, might be able to tell me who went through the gate around the times of each crime. My experience as a reporter suggested there was much I didn't know yet, a lot more rocks to look under, several clues big and small, and even more information I'd have to sort through and ignore to eliminate as clues. But I had a place to start. Some threads. I'd just need to pull on them, see what unraveled.

That was all I'd needed to work out for now. I reached

an outcropping that marked the two-mile point, turned around and looked down the trail. I felt good, decided today would be a six-miler. I turned and headed up the steeper part of the mountain to put in another mile, fell back into my pace, and willed my mind to focus on nothing but breathing and footsteps, breathing and footsteps.

CHAPTER 6

J ack Beachum had been a cop most of his adult life. In his early seventies now, he'd joined the Pleasant Sheriff's Posse, a group of a dozen men of varying age, but mostly not spring chickens, who had all the clout a uniform implied, without the authority to go with it. He could spot a crime, but regulations required he call it in and wait for the real deputies to arrive and take over. Mostly he directed traffic during the annual Veteran's Day Parade and guided school kids at a crosswalk each morning. Sometimes he got bored doing only that.

Jack Beachum and I were best friends. Neither of us had ever said so.

"Morning, Beach."

Beach was sitting at his usual table on the patio of Lulu's Grind, the coffee shop on the northeast corner of the town center, not two-hundred feet from Ringo, the two-hundred-year-old saguaro that sat in the middle of the traffic circle where Pleasant Way and Happy Lane met. It was the site of an infamous, brief, non-lethal shootout back in 1881, which left a bullet imbedded in the cactus and a big mystery surrounding who had really shot at Johnny Ringo. Locals said it was Doc Holliday, but some experts disagreed. Nobody was injured, so the shootout wasn't as widely known as ones like the OK Corral. But it was a big deal in Pleasant lore.

Beach unfolded his six-foot frame, stood, and gave me his customary firm handshake. We exchanged good mornings. Beach was about an inch shorter than me, and I noticed only because he always seemed to try and stretch himself tall so our eyes would be nearly level. Like me, he had broad shoulders. That's where the similarities ended. Beach had giant calves, thick thighs and outsized forearms. I considered myself muscular compared to the average male, but if I were a running back, Beach would be the blocking fullback who powered open the holes for me. He wore his usual tan posse pants and tan short-sleeve button-up shirt, which matched his hair color. Pants and shirt neatly pressed. Straight hair neatly cropped, the front pushing forward but too short to be called bangs.

He sat back down, folded his arms, leaned his chair back against the outer wall of the Grind, and adjusted his black leather belt loaded with posse stuff. His 9 mm was holstered. On his right shoulder was a blue and yellow sheriff's patch, complementing the metal star on his left breast.

I pulled out a chair, turned it around, and sat on it backward. "Shoot anybody today?"

"What do you want," Beach said, not gruffly, just matter-of-factly. Jack Beachum was from Texas, and one thing he never did was beat around the bush. With his left fist he gently and rhythmically squeezed a red rubber ball, the type used in racquetball.

"Who says I want something?"

"It's generally why you offer to buy this old geezer a coffee. I have a meeting in twenty minutes, official sheriff stuff, so I figured we might skip the small talk today and get right to it. What's up?"

"Well, I really just wanted coffee. But since you ask," I lowered my voice and leaned forward, rocking the chair onto its back legs, "I'm interested in the Bernstein murder."

Lulu herself came out and walked up to the table. She was Tanzanian, about five-seven and thin with short-cropped hair and dark, wrinkle-free skin. She might have been in her twenties, but when she smiled, which was often, creases around her eyes suggested she might be forty. It was a mystery the regulars all talked about. Even Jess, who had been her best friend, didn't know how old Lulu was. Lulu let the mystery be. She was apparently single, spoke with a thick accent, was always in a good mood, and was sexy as hell. Nobody ever wondered why Lulu's Grind was usually busy, even though three Starbucks were within four miles. People actually drove from Scottsdale and other surrounding smaller towns regularly just to visit Lulu's in Pleasant, where the coffee was rumored to be a Tanzanian tribal secret, the omelets were five-star-restaurant quality, and the homemade pastries might've been FedExed in from Paris each day.

"What *you* boys want today?" Lulu asked, her smile a mile wide, showing white teeth that were just imperfect enough—a mild overbite and one top front tooth crossing the other slightly—to make her even sexier.

I leaned back and admired Lulu's smile. I looked at Beach, who was clearly enjoying Lulu's smile even more. "Two coffees for here," I said. At Lulu's, you didn't ask for caramel or mocha or frappe-anything. There was no grande, no tall. It was coffee, with or without cream and sugar. To stay or to go.

"No breakfast? Not even pastry?"

"Not today," I said. "Beach is in a hurry, has to go arrest somebody."

"Long as it's not me," Lulu said. "Be right back with coffee."

After Lulu was back inside, Beach finally shifted his attention back to me. "You looking into Tinker Bernstein's murder for the paper? I thought you weren't working these days. Anyway, your friend Sam and the other reporters all been around, we told 'em most everything we know. Case not closed."

"Actually, Delores Bernstein hired me."

"What the hay…what do you mean?"

"Sam told her I might be able to help find her husband's killer."

"What, you a dick now?"

"I think I prefer *private eye*. Yeah, I guess. Sam suggested it. It's something to do. I thought I'd try it out."

"Don't matter what you prefer. Jesus. Eli Quinn a private detective, huh?" Beach looked around at the other tables, put his hands behind his head and leaned back, switched the rubber ball into his right hand and gave it a few slow, hard squeezes. "Son of a gun. Makes sense, actually. You're a tenacious bastard when you start digging into something. You know you need a license, right?"

"I haven't looked into that yet."

"What you need is a Private Investigator Employee registration certificate, which proves you work for a sponsoring agency, or you need a Private Investigation Agency license."

"Sounds like a bunch of hoops. What's that actually mean?"

"In your case, means you need to convince the state you been doing this for three years, get a license to run your own agency, 'fore you can hang out a shingle."

"Or?"

"Or you could just go ahead and play detective, and maybe get slapped with a misdemeanor charge."

"Or?"

"Don't know any other 'ors.' I guess maybe you do really good on your first case, some strings might get pulled and a few technicalities ignored. But I can't advise you to do that, me being just a posse member and all."

Pleasant didn't have its own law enforcement, relying instead on a contract with the Maricopa County Sheriff's Office. There was a little substation in Pleasant, right across the street from Lulu's Grind, facing the traffic circle and Ringo, the saguaro. The contract called for one sheriff deputy to always be in town, manning the substation or driving around doing whatever sheriff deputies did in a relatively quiet town. Beyond that one person, the posse members did a lot of the routine police work in town.

***

"So what can you tell me about the Bernstein case," I asked my friend.

"Not a lot that you haven't read in the papers," Beach said. "I'm not on the case, of course. I'm never really on a case. But I've heard a few things. What do you want to know?"

"Any leads at all?"

"Nope."

"Any hunches?"

"Nada."

"Any clues that point to a motive?"

"Zilch."

"Anything you're not telling me?"

"Wouldn't tell you if there was."

"You're a fount of knowledge, Beach."

Lulu brought two coffees. We both leaned back, smiled at her. She put the coffee down, we thanked her, and she left. We sipped.

"If we had anything to go on, we'd be pursuing it," Beach said. "And I might tell you about it."

"You know you would," I said. We both smiled at the shared truth. Beach trusted me, and I never betrayed him by letting anyone know where my tips came from. I said, "So we got nothing."

41

"Please don't say we."

"OK fine. *I* got nothing. What are you going to do to help your friend?"

"This private detecting thing ain't so easy, huh?"

I thought for a minute. We both drank some coffee.

I asked, "What about the wife?"

"Delores? Yeah, technically she's the only suspect. Technically she doesn't have an alibi. The clock thing is strange, and you could read that to mean it looks like she set things up. But there's no murder weapon, and no motive other than the insurance policy. Thing is, I know Delores, and I don't think she did it."

"People always say that."

"Yeah, but those people aren't always posse."

"And being on the posse, you're a trained observer of people."

"Gotta be an elite individual to join the posse."

"I hear you have to be at least eighteen, in good physical and mental condition," I said.

"And no criminal record."

"Tough standards."

"Don't know how I got in."

"Probably because you're eighteen times about four. That gave you a fourfold advantage on one quarter of the requirements."

"That and I don't need the money."

"I thought the posse was all volunteer."

"That's the money I'm talking about. You need some, you're disqualified."

"What are there, twelve posse in town now?"

"Yep, after the last recruitment meeting, two more kids signed up, couple guys in their sixties. Pleasant got more lawmen per capita than any other town in America."

"That true?"

"No clue. But it sounds good and probably ain't far from the truth, so we say it now. We'll wait for somebody to call the bluff and prove us wrong."

"Let me try a tangent," I said.

"Big word."

"I'm a walking dictionary. This maybe has nothing to do with anything. But the security system at the gate. How come they take down your license number, when they've got a camera snaps a picture of it?"

"You've been detecting."

"Actually, I just paid attention when I went up there the other day."

"Lotta people don't."

"Not everyone owns a Private Investigator Agency."

"Or hopes to," Beach said. He leaned in and spoke lower. "Camera wasn't working."

"Since when?"

"Since about two weeks before the murder."

"Well that sounds suspiciously like a clue, or at least something to look into. Why'd it take so long to fix the camera?"

"You remember the security gate used to be run by the Pleasant town council. A few years back, they contracted the work out to Dribbs Security. When the camera broke, Dribbs said it was council's camera, council said it's Dribbs' camera. They argued until Tinker Bernstein was killed, then apparently agreed to split the cost and get it fixed lickety-split."

"Lickety-split?"

Beach ignored me. "A new one was installed the other day. Meantime, while the camera was out, they recorded each license plate manually. Now they still do that as routine backup."

"So they have a record of what time Delores Bernstein came back through the gate."

"6:48."

"Enough time to get home, murder her husband at 6:59."

43

"Just."

"You guys run the list on who else came in before the murder?"

Beach drank some coffee while rolling his eyes. "Course. We look like amateurs?"

"No, but you're old. Maybe you forget basic procedure."

My friend bounced the rubber ball once on the patio, hard, and it came right back to his hand. "Not my procedures anyway," he said. "You know they don't let us posse guys do any investigating. But yeah, they looked back to first thing that morning. Every plate was either a homeowner, an invited guest who was OKed by a homeowner, or a known contractor."

"Contractor?"

"UPS, FedEx, guys like that. A few landscapers that come regularly."

"So nobody suspicious?"

"I don't know the details, but I hear they checked a couple that might've been a wee bit suspect, alibies were solid. Dead ends."

"So whoever killed Tinker Bernstein," I said, "was either a country club resident…"

"Unlikely, but we found a few friends and acquaintances out of that list of fifteen hundred people and interviewed them. That went nowhere. Been pretty quiet up there for what, ten years now?"

"Or one of their guests…"

"Also unlikely. We did run a couple down who had priors. But nothing serious."

"Or a contractor who's been there before…"

"More likely, but we didn't find any motives, and we found good alibies."

"Or someone snuck in."

"That'd be my bet," Beach said.

I nodded. He finished his coffee and pushed himself up.

"Professional job?" I asked.

"Hard to say. But that's a good question. There were two bullets. Coroner can't be sure, but he thinks the one to the forehead was first, and that's what killed Tinker. The other one, to the chest, looked to have been fired when he was already lying on his back. The bullet was embedded in the concrete right underneath him."

"So the second shot wasn't necessary."

"And pros don't like to waste bullets. Leaves more evidence. Is messy. Pros pride themselves on doing it in one shot."

"But two shots might not be a total amateur, either."

"Right," Beach said. "If the killer didn't expect Bernstein to be there, and he were surprised, he might fire several shots, miss a couple times. But Bernstein took one to the forehead, apparently while sitting in his chair. That doesn't sound to me like a run-of-the-mill burglar got surprised."

"What kind of gun?"

"Can't be sure. We know the caliber, but we'd need a gun to match it to. Silencer, they figure, since there were neighbors at home and nobody heard anything."

"So it's someone who probably knows how to use a gun, given the precision of the head shot and the clock shot. Someone who has a silencer, has probably been in some shady situations before, but isn't a top-tier hired shooter. Probably not a jealous lover from the country club."

"That was roughly our profile, yeah," Beach said. "And that's where we ended up. Nothing else pointed anywhere. The deputies didn't tell Bernstein's wife all the details. She's still a suspect. Can't give away all our big clues. The case folder is still on someone's desk, but it probably hasn't been opened the past day or so, and by end of week it'll be in a file cabinet. sheriff will have a couple more press conferences after that and say everything possible is being done, but in reality the manpower will be shifted to other cases."

We each looked at our coffees. Beach had stopped

working the ball. It was never pleasant to talk about a murder. Even though it was our jobs to talk about Bernstein being shot in the forehead, a little silence seemed in order.

***

"Solo looks good," Beach said, breaking the silence and looking over at the dog in the red Jeep, who was looking back at us.

"Always," I said. It was Jack Beachum who'd brought Solo to me. Shortly after Jess was killed, the sheriff's K-9 unit had a dog that needed a new home. Solo had made it through all the training and knew how to chase a suspect, growl ferociously, and hold the suspect. But ultimately he was deemed unfit for service. He performed all the tasks well, but had two flaws. He often intuited situations and moved in before his handler commanded him to do so. More often than not Solo was right, and he'd make a beeline for the acting "bad guy," but in the K-9 unit, discipline was not negotiable. Also, Solo wasn't much of a barker. He would let out one intimidating bark at the first recognition of a situation, but then relied on his deep growl. The growl was plenty effective up close, but the Bark and Hold training method relied on a lot of barking. Barking alone scared the crap out of criminals, before the dog even got close, and sometimes they'd just put their guns down and freeze a block away. The K-9 unit had a lot of good dogs to choose from, and they didn't need a loose cannon or a non-barker in their ranks.

"Not a bad companion in your new line of work," Beach said. "Be careful. He's an eager one. Could cause you trouble."

"I'm not worried. He always seems to know exactly what to do, before I tell him."

"But he hasn't been truly challenged, in a real situation, where you might need him to corner a creep and avoid mauling an innocent citizen. Or who knows what."

"He's not going to maul any innocent citizens. If something comes up, I think he'll know what to do. And if he doesn't, he'll do what I tell him."

"I think you're right," Beach said. "Helluva dog."

"Yep. I owe you one. And thanks for the information today, too."

"I'll put it on the tab."

CHAPTER 7

I called Samantha Marcos on her cell.

"Hey, you," she said.

"Hey, it's me," I said, even though her phone had already clued her in. "Did you know Steve Wynn sold Picasso's *Le Rêve* to Steven Cohen for more than $155 million a couple years back? And that was after Wynn had accidentally put his elbow through the painting."

"Steve Wynn, the casino owner?"

"Yep, that Steve Wynn. And Cézanne's *Card Players* was sold by an individual to the Qatar government in 2011 for more than $250 million."

"Qatar bought a Cézanne?"

"They have a lot of money in Qatar," I said. "Almost as much as Steve Wynn."

"And you're telling me this because ..."

"Fortunes can be made buying and selling art."

"Ah, I see," she said. "Or stealing it."

"Exactly. Tinker Bernstein didn't collect the most expensive paintings, but there's plenty to be made buying less famous works. And there's a ton of shady stuff goes on, too."

"Tell me."

"Seven paintings were stolen from some museum in Europe in 2012. There was a Monet, a Picasso and a Matisse in the mix. Same year, a Warhol was among nineteen pieces lifted from a private collection in Detroit. Thefts like this occur every year. Fewer than ten percent are ever recovered. Apparently there's no trouble unloading pieces on the black market. They don't have to get anywhere near market value to rake in some big money. And the art doesn't even have to be legit. A while back a woman was caught hawking fake paintings, forged by a Chinese immigrant who was proficient at copying the Modernist masters. He painted in Queens. She sold them through a gallery in Manhattan. She made something like $33 million over the years, and the gallery made even more. The painter got screwed."

"They often do."

"He was paid in the thousands for each forgery."

"OK, got it," Sam said. "But nothing was stolen from Tinker Bernstein's collection."

"Nothing we know of."

"You think maybe there was a painting Delores didn't know about?"

"I don't know," I said. And I didn't. But it was a decent hunch, I figured, that the pair of Bernstein crimes might be related somehow to art. "But if there was, and the thieves thought she might not know about it, then killing Bernstein might've been a way to keep the sheriff off their tail, at least for a while. For all I know, maybe Delores took it herself."

"All sounds a little far-fetched. You're going to need some more information. Clues. That's what you need. Clues."

"Yeah, I'm looking. Know any art thieves?"

"Personally, no," she said. "What do you have in mind?"

"If I can find some, I'll poke around. Ask questions. Maybe make somebody nervous. I interviewed the close friends of the Bernsteins this morning, including Charlie

Entwill, Tinker's golf buddy. I learned roughly nothing. I need to go in a different direction, and if there was some sort of art theft involved, I want to move quickly. The longer this goes, the greater chance the evidence, if there is any, gets sold and shipped who knows where."

"So you're going to find a couple known art thieves, ask questions, and hope they happen to know something about this case. Sounds like a shot in the dark."

"I got nothing else."

"Doing something is better than doing nothing," she said.

"And maybe if I find somebody who wasn't involved, but knows about stuff like this, they can point me somewhere. Or if I just shake the tree, maybe word'll get around and a bad apple will fall out somewhere."

"The apple analogy isn't working for me."

"I'll lose that. Thanks. Meantime I'm going to go see Delores again, learn a little more about Tinker's art collection, get a better feel for her. You at the paper?"

Even though The Republic ran with an online-first mentality, everyone still called it "the paper."

"Yep," Sam said. "I'll see what I can find out in our *Art Thieves in Pleasant* archives. I guess this makes me a sidekick. Shall we discuss the evidence over lunch?"

"Sure," I said. "I'll call you when I leave the country club. I met with Beach this morning, too, and he told me something really interesting. I'll fill you in. Meet you at Amir's?"

"You don't want to take me to the Clubhouse Grill?"

"On my new salary, I can't afford their water, let alone the BLT."

"It tastes like crap anyway," Sam said. "And other than you and me, it'd be a stuffy crowd."

"We have similar tastes," I said. I wished I hadn't said it. It was starting to sound like a date. I hoped Sam didn't think of it as a date. I wished I didn't think of it that way. Or maybe we both wished it were a date. Before I could dwell on the idea any longer, Sam said "Bye" and clicked off.

CHAPTER 8

"Hello, Mrs. Bernstein," I said as she opened her front door.

"Delores, please," she said.

"Thank you for seeing me, Delores." She'd beaten me down on the formalities issue.

"I hired you. Of course I'll see you," she said matter-of-factly. "Please come in. Can I get you something to drink? Water, coffee? Something stronger?"

"Some coffee would be great," I said, though I was fully coffeed up and didn't need any, and something stronger sounded good. The house was cool again. At least the coffee would feel good in my hands. I could wait and have a drink later.

While she made coffee in the kitchen, I walked around the living room and inspected the paintings. Didn't recognize any of them. Didn't even recognize any of the signatures. That didn't mean some of them weren't famous. My knowledge of art didn't extend very far beyond comics, a couple well-known living photographers like Art Wolfe and Annie Leibovitz, and a handful of dead painters I was made to study in school.

Delores returned with two coffees in white ceramic cups on the same tray, set it on the coffee table. She sat down on the Queen Ann. She was wearing a long-sleeved blue crinkle-neck top with a simple knit pattern, loose black slacks and black flats. Simple and sensible again, without being unconscious of fashion.

I thanked her, then started my inquiry. I tried to sound like I knew what I was doing.

"There's just one entrance to the country club, and I'm told nobody gets in unless they're an invited guest, or are working for some contractor like FedEx or a hired contractor. Have you had any work done on the house recently?"

"Tinker hired a handyman to redo the back wall there," she said, pointing at the wall of windows beyond the living and dining area. "It had small windows, and a big view, so he had the whole wall blown out. The contractor put a giant beam in, with a post in the middle, then rebuilt the wall with as little wall and as much window as possible."

"When was this?"

"He finished a couple months ago."

"So this guy was in your house for what, several days?"

"Two weeks, off and on."

"Do you remember his name?"

"Of course. J.D. Fish. A local contractor. Nice man."

"Did you mention this to the sheriff deputies?"

"Well, no," she said. "They didn't ask."

"Potentially important, don't you think?"

"Frankly, no," she said. "J.D. is a good person. We've known him since we moved here. Tinker had him help with several projects. Tinker was good with mechanical stuff, but he couldn't pound a nail straight to save his life. He called J.D. whenever there was carpentry, or anything that was just too big or heavy for one person to handle."

"You have J.D.'s card?" After she fetched it in the kitchen, I looked at it: *J.D. Fish, Handyman.* The phone number was inside the outline of a fish, with an address below that, and a boldface italic line at the bottom: *You want it, I build it.* I wasn't sure if it was a Jesus fish, or just a fish.

"You don't really think J.D. had anything to do with this."

"I have no clue," I said. "Almost literally. I'll visit him, ask him a few questions. Do me a favor and don't tell him about me."

"You want to surprise him."

"Yes."

"See how he reacts."

"Yes."

"Be nice to him."

"I promise," I said. "As long as he's nice to me."

I put the card in my pocket. "The night your husband was killed, you came through the gate at 6:48. He was apparently shot at 6:59, according to the clock."

"You still suspect me, Mr. Quinn."

"I'm just looking at all the facts," I said. "What you hired me to do."

"Very well."

"Does that timing sound right to you?"

"I suppose," she said. "I really don't know exactly what time I came through the gate. I would have guessed a bit later than that, but if they say 6:48, then sure, that sounds about right. All I know is the sun was about to set, so I went and watched it go down."

"How long did it take to get from the gate to the place where you watched the sunset?"

"I don't know. Maybe five minutes."

"I'll check the distance and time in my Jeep," I said. "I looked up the sunset time. 7:05 that night. Did you wait long for it to set after you got there?"

"A few minutes."

"And did you watch it for long, after it set?"

"Several minutes."

"So that would put you back at the house around what, maybe 7:15 or 7:20?

"That sounds about right. I didn't pay close attention to the time. There was no reason to."

"Nobody saw you after you came through the gate, before you got home?"

"No."

She was being helpful, answering a lot of questions. Maybe that was a good sign. I didn't know. I had more questions, so I just kept going. "OK, so tell me about some of these paintings. I'd like to know what they're worth."

"Does that mean I'm no longer a suspect?"

"It means I've asked all the questions I can think of about the sunset and the clock and the time of death. Honestly, Delores, I don't make you for a murderer, but your lack of an alibi is a problem. You hired me, but I'm a pretty smart guy, and I have my own reputation at stake here on this first case, so I'm being thorough. The more I understand, the better chance I have of solving it. Right now, I don't understand much of anything, so all I can do is keep asking questions, see where the answers go."

Delores stood, and I followed her to a black and white, cut-paper silhouette. "That's a Kara Walker," she said. "Tinker paid $250,000 for it a few years ago." To me it looked like something you'd find in a public domain stock art book, but I didn't say so.

"He picked up that delightful Winslow Homer sketch for $120,000 last year. It's one of my favorites." It was a lightly drawn sketch of two girls walking in a field. I guessed "minimalist" would be the word to best describe it. I liked it.

Delores pointed out several other pieces by artists I had never heard of, mostly six figures, a few worth less.

"Did it ever occur to you, to Mr. Bernstein ..."

"Tinker. Please call him Tinker."

"Did it ever occur to you and Tinker to lock all this art up?"

"We talked about it. But Tinker always just wanted to enjoy it. And he did. Often he'd walk around the living room like it were a gallery, inspecting each piece at a distance, then up close. It brought him great joy. Anyway, what should he do, put them in a safe deposit box? Or lock them in a closet? We live in a gated community, the house has an alarm, and we're not overly social. Not many folks know who we are or where we live, or what's in our house."

Looking around the room, I noted that she still sometimes spoke in the present tense about her husband. I understood. Took me months before I could speak of Jess in the past tense. I got up, took the cup of coffee, walked up to one of the paintings, an abstract piece that might have represented a building, or maybe a rock outcropping. I inspected it as if something profound might occur to me. Nothing did. So I moved to the left where the bust of Ben Franklin sat perched, a little precariously I thought, on the narrow pedestal. He looked a lot like the image on the hundred-dollar bill—bald on top but with long, stringy hair that had a greasy, hippy-like quality that eccentric geezers are often excused for. But this sculpted Benjamin seemed older.

"He looks sad," I said. "Or tired."

"Interesting," Delores said. "Tinker said this Franklin looked thoughtful, distinguished."

Kindred spirits. Franklin was an inventor—everything from the lightning rod to bifocals to swim fins. A tinkerer for sure.

"I imagine your husband felt a kinship with Franklin," I said.

"That's why he bought it. He called the piece *The Tinkerer*. An unofficial title, but if you buy a piece, you can bestow upon it whatever title you wish, I guess. I still can't believe he bought it—it cost a fortune."

"You mind I ask how much?" I sipped the coffee.

"He paid two-point-five million for it. He said it's

probably worth about three now. More than anything else in the house."

I almost spit coffee on the bust. "Three million dollars? Really?"

"Really. It's a 1778 piece by French sculptor Jean-Antoine Houdon. I only know that because Tinker told me. It was actually stolen a few years back, from a home in Philadelphia, by the maid, and when it was recovered, the owner had it appraised and auctioned it off."

"And here it sits, in plain sight, after you were broken into twice." I looked around the room again. "Lots of expensive art just sitting here."

"Tinker bought most of this anonymously through an agent, so as far as we know, nobody but a few close friends even knows the bust or any of this is here, or that it's worth anything."

"Still…"

"You think it's a clue."

"Unfortunately, I have no idea," I admitted. "It's just an interesting item of note for now. But I won't be surprised if there is a clue in this room somewhere."

CHAPTER 9

There was no better food in Pleasant than at Café Amir. Because a town ordinance prohibited chain restaurants, Café Amir didn't have to compete with TGI Fridays or Burger King. There would have been no competition on taste or quality, but in other small towns, the chains drew so much business they made it difficult for an entrepreneur to survive. This was why Amir Yalda opened his restaurant in the center of Pleasant. It was diagonally opposite Lulu's Grind on the southwest side of the traffic circle, where Pleasant Way and Happy Lane met. If you drew a line from Café Amir to Lulu's, it would cut right through Ringo, the saguaro with the bullet in it.

I parked the Jeep across the street. Solo bounded from the back seat and followed me to the cafe. I was in my new detective outfit: jeans, loafers and T-shirt. Like any good detective, I packed a holstered iPhone on my right hip.

At the low wrought-iron fence surrounding the patio, I said, "Down." Solo lied down, but remained attentive, ready to spring into action if necessary. Meantime he'd stay put, content to see, hear and smell everything, registering more detail than any good detective, and always keeping half an eye on me.

It was hard to get a table during lunch or dinner at Café Amir. There were plenty of tables at two in the afternoon. I picked one outside, in the shade of the two-story building that housed the café and, above it, Amir and his family.

It was hotter today, in the high-nineties, but still dry. I liked the heat. And we'd have privacy on the patio. To talk about the case. That's how I justified the table selection to myself.

The town was quiet. Kids were in school, adults at work. A few cars came through, slowing as they navigated the traffic circle, which still had the original cobblestones set in place back in 1913.

Sam parked next to the Jeep. She wore black jeans and a simple white V-neck T-shirt. Black flats with no socks, a single silver bracelet on her left wrist. I noticed all this only because I was in detective mode.

She said hello to Solo first. Solo put his paws up on her thighs, and Sam scratched behind his ears.

"I see it's a double date," she said.

"Nah," I said. "Solo already ate." I stood, looking at Sam. "Sit," I said. I was still looking at Sam, but Solo sat, which was what I meant to have happen. I was still looking at Sam, until I realized that the looking had turned into staring. She curled a bit of hair behind her ear and looked away. I mentally kicked myself for staring. Then I looked at Solo and commanded him to lie down. Sam came through the gate and sat across from me, and we talked briefly about what a beautiful day it was. We had a way of putting the awkward moments behind us and getting back to our friendship, or our work.

Amir came to the table and greeted us warmly. "Hello, Ms. Marcos. Mr. Quinn." Amir was always formal, despite the fact we were old friends. "I hear about the case."

I'm sure the smile dropped noticeably from my face. Sam had been distracting me from trial of Jess' murderer, if only for a day.

"The scumbag is guilty," Amir said. "Is good."

"Yes," I said, nodding without enthusiasm.

"Good," Amir said. "Is finish."

I nodded again, but that's all I had. There was an awkward silence. "Your server is right out," he said. "Good to see both of you. Enjoy lunch. Can I get anything?"

"No, thank you," I said.

Amir smiled and walked backward a couple steps, a custom of his, before turning and retreating to the kitchen.

"He cares about you, is all," Sam said.

"I know. I'm trying to move forward, but each time someone brings it up, I get pulled back. I can't help my reaction."

"No, you can't. So let's take a step forward. Bring me up to speed on the case."

"I had a really interesting talk with Jack Beachum this morning."

"How's Beach?"

"Same-same. Still in shape. Still sharp. Doesn't take any crap. He says the security camera wasn't working at the time of the murder. Hadn't been for a couple weeks."

"Which would explain why they wrote down your license plate number when we went to see Delores yesterday."

"Yeah. They have a new camera now, but while it was out, they were taking numbers down manually. Now they do it as backup. New procedure."

"You thinking that could have something to do with the case."

"It's something to noodle."

"Manual systems involve humans. Humans are fallible. Might've provided an opportunity," she said.

"Might've. We don't have a motive, but now we have a possible means."

"Is that detective talk?"

"Darn tootin."

"You've been hanging around Beach too much."

A new waitress came out with menus. She set the menus down. Neither of us looked at the menus.

"I think we can order," Sam said.

"What can I get you?" the waitress asked. Her ponytail bounced when she talked.

"We'll have the baba ghanoush appetizer, tabbouleh and some hummus," Sam said. "And please bring extra pita."

The waitress didn't write anything down, but she had the order.

"Anything else?" She addressed at me. I watched Sam watch the waitress watch me. Interesting.

"Let's get some chicken shawarma, too," I said.

"That's not on the menu anymore," the waitress said, politely.

"I know," I said. "Ask Amir though. He'll make it."

Her ponytail bobbed in a friendly way, as she shifted her weight from one foot to the other, revealing impatience. "I can try," she said.

"And some of that cucumber stuff," I said. "Yogurt and cucumber. I can never remember what it's called."

The ponytail swung to the other side as the waitress shifted feet again. She didn't say anything. She looked at Sam.

"Tzatziki," Sam said. I nodded. Sam knew it was one of my favorites. It came with different ingredients and different flavors at various Mediterranean restaurants around the Valley. Amir frequently claimed his, made with lemon, not vinegar, and just a hint of mint, was preferable to the Greek style. I couldn't argue.

I also ordered a Sierra Nevada. "You want one?

"I don't drink during the day," Sam said.

"Neither do I," I looked at my watch. "It's quarter after five in New York City."

"I love New York," Sam said.

"We can pretend we're there," I said.

"Oh, what the hell," Sam said. The waitress thanked us, picked up the menus and left.

Sam asked: "Learn anything new from Delores?"

"I quizzed her about the timing of it all. She came through the gate at 6:48, according to the records. Tinker is shot at 6:59, according to the dead clock. Sunset was at 7:05, according to the U.S. Naval Observatory web site. That last one is the only time I trust."

"You think the time she entered the gate could have been wrong?"

"By accident or on purpose," I said.

"And the clock?"

"Leaning toward believing that one as the time of death. I don't see a reason to have shot it at any other time. But I just don't know."

"So Delores remains a suspect," she said.

"For now. But I'm coming around to your view, that there's something screwy. The more I look into the art, the more I figure it must've played a role. They've got several paintings worth stealing. A bunch are worth six figures. One's worth almost a million bucks. And one item is worth even more. Wanna guess?"

"I know at least as much about art as you," she said. "So, let me see." She looked up into a corner of her brain, held her chin and tapped a finger on her upper lip. "I give."

"The Franklin bust. It's from the 1700s, French sculptor named Jean-Antoine Houdini or something. And get this: It was stolen before. In Philly. They got it back and the owner decided to unload. Bernstein bought it anonymously at auction. Delores said they have always been very quiet about the art collection. Only close friends knew about any of it."

"All of which might mean nothing," Sam said, "because we're still operating under the assumption that no art was taken, right?"

"That's one assumption."

The waitress delivered our Sierra Nevadas. I took a long

pull from the bottle. Sam poured hers into a glass and had a sip.

"Delores would've noticed a missing piece," Sam said.

"If it were obviously missing."

"What are you thinking?"

"I don't know," I said.

"That doesn't sound like detecting."

"Hell, it's not even guessing yet," I said. "Just feels like something doesn't add up. I mean, a guy is murdered in his home in the country club, a gated community, for no apparent reason. Three days earlier, his PC is stolen. Maybe there was something valuable on the PC."

"Like what?"

"No clue," I said.

"Pretty soon you have to stop saying that."

"Maybe he had some valuable trade secrets from GE."

"Trade secrets worth stealing," Sam said, "then worth killing for to make sure the previous owner didn't talk about it, so whoever stole them didn't get caught."

"Maybe."

"That's not a bad hunch," Sam said. "Why didn't you think of that earlier?"

"Because I just thought of it now. If I'd thought of it earlier, maybe we wouldn't have needed lunch together in New York. And then maybe I'd never have gotten the chance to come up with it and you wouldn't have had a beer in the afternoon."

"That makes no sense," she said.

"Like this case."

"Well, the good news is, your detective skills are improving daily."

"It's been two days."

"Yeah, but if you can sustain the momentum, pretty soon you'll be able to solve anything. Get you a reality show."

I huffed. Neither of us wasted our time on reality TV. It

was a running joke between us that the supposed pinnacle of any career is to get your own reality show.

The waitress delivered hummus, tabbouleh, baba ghanoush and tzatziki. I took a second long pull from the beer, nearly finished it. Tilted it toward the waitress to signal another. Sam took another sip of hers. She tore a large piece of pita and dipped it into the baba ghanoush, took small bites.

"There's one new twist," I said. "Delores just told me about this contractor, J.D. Fish, who has done work for Tinker off and on over the years. He recently tore the back of the house off, rebuilt it with those big windows."

"Great view. I can't believe it wasn't all windows before."

"It's probably nothing, but if anyone can slip in and out of the country club easily, it'd be a local contractor. Plus we still haven't ruled Delores out. They could be in cahoots."

"Cahoots."

"Detective talk."

"Yeah, OK. So you think it's worth talking to this Fish guy," she said.

"I think so."

"Have some baba ghanoush," she said. "It's exquisite."

"He does know how to make baba ghanoush. Just enough lemon, not too much garlic. And he uses fresh olive oil. That gives it the slight burn in the back of your throat."

"How do you know all this?"

"I watched him make it one day. I make a good baba ghanoush, but there was always something missing. He'd told me his recipe, but it wasn't the same. So I watched him, and he was using a brand of olive oil I'd never heard of."

"You have to use extra virgin," Sam said. "Everybody knows that."

"Yeah, but it turns out most olive oil takes months to get from the tree to the table, and it loses flavor and nutrients. So you have to find really fresh olive oil, and only a few manufacturers actually date stamp it."

"So you can make this baba ghanoush at home?"

"I can."

"You'll have to show me sometime."

"I will."

A brief silence settled between us. We were comfortable quiet, and it was one of the reasons we'd become friends. This time it felt maybe a little less comfortable than others. Or a little more comfortable. I wasn't sure. So I pushed my brain to get back to the case.

My second beer and the shawarma arrived. I looked at the beer. I looked at Sam's glass, still more than half full. I summoned a bunch of willpower and let my beer sit.

"So. What'd *you* find out?" I asked, still watching the beer. "Any art thieves in our midst?" I spooned a healthy amount of tzatziki on pita and took a big bite.

"There's a couple guys in county jail that did some high-profile residential thefts around the Valley. One involved some paintings, but nothing particularly valuable. The other was mostly into jewelry and had stolen one painting. Neither sounded anything like what happened in country club. I didn't try to learn too much about them regardless, since they're in jail and probably didn't kill Tinker Bernstein."

"Good call. Given what I'm paying you, I can't have you chasing wild gooses."

"There's another guy pretty interesting. Bobby Gonzales, aka Bobby G. He's suspected of a few high-profile art thefts but there hadn't been any good evidence. Then he and an accomplice, big Slavic guy named Radu something-or-other, made a daring theft several years ago in Detroit. They ripped off seven really expensive paintings from a collector's home. Maybe would've gotten away with it, but a butler who wasn't supposed to be there, was. Radu shot him. Looks like he meant to kill him, but it was sloppy gun work. Radu was known for being muscle, not a shooter. Butler survives, identifies both of them. Bobby G gets seven years. Radu is still in.

"And I'm guessing Bobby G isn't living in Detroit any more," I said. I drank some beer, but not a lot.

"Scottsdale," Sam said.

"How'd you find all that?"

"Some of it was in the AP archives," she said. "But I've got an FBI friend who sometimes fills in some details for me."

"Friend?"

"Used to be a boyfriend."

"What happened?"

"He got offered a job in DC, Art Theft Crime Team."

"They have that?"

"Yep. He said the trafficking in stolen art and other cultural property runs into the billions of dollars annually. They get involved whenever things cross state lines or go out of the country. Anyway, he moved. I stayed. Long-distance thing didn't work, but we stayed friends."

We were both quiet a couple minutes, eating. Sam sipped her beer. I drank mine. We ate. I tried to telepathically glean if she still had feelings for this FBI guy. But Sam's ability to block telepathy was apparently strong.

"Good friend to have," I finally said. She tilted her head, shrugged with a tiny grin. "So this Bobby G. He been clean since he got out?"

"FBI doesn't have any reason to think otherwise," she said. "But thieves like him rarely reform."

"Is that your professional psychologist's opinion?"

"I'm not a professional psychologist."

"You've got a master's degree."

"Didn't get the Ph.D. Never went into practice."

"The lure of riches in journalism was just too strong."

Sam just shook her head at that one.

"So there was a break-in down in Paradise Valley a couple months ago," she said. "Some former NBA player had three LeRoy Neiman's stolen."

"LeRoy Neiman? The guy with the big handlebar mustache who painted sports celebrities? Didn't he die recently?"

"Couple years ago," she said. "He was ninety-one."

"His paintings worth anything?"

"Not exactly Picasso prices. But they're easy to fence, my guy said. A lot of people who might want one would be less likely to be thorough about authentication, might not ask many questions. So a thief could turn some quick cash. Thing is, the way it happened looked like Bobby G's M.O."

"And what's your guy say that would look like?"

"Owner's collection wasn't widely known. Bad guys appeared to have some inside information that told them what was there and when nobody would be there. Only the most valuable pieces were stolen. In each one, a TV was ripped off to make it look like it wasn't just an art theft. Only difference is in the Paradise Valley theft, nobody was shot, and there were no witnesses, no other evidence."

"They got nothing on Bobby G."

"Nothing but a hunch."

"They pay him a visit?"

"Nope," she said. "Figured it's better to not let on they're thinking about him. See if he tries another one, maybe trips himself up."

"They mind if I pay Bobby G a visit?"

"I figured you'd ask, so I asked. Not a problem, as long as you don't mention anything I've told you."

"Let's just say, and I'm spitballing here, that Bobby G is our guy," I said.

"I'll call that a long shot."

"Helluva," I said. "But let's just say."

"My guy doesn't think so."

"Your guy have a name?"

"Yep." She smiled.

I waited, pushed a little food around on my plate. She didn't say anything else. "Your guy say the Feds looked into

Bernstein's murder?"

"Nope. He hadn't heard of it until I mentioned it. He said the stolen TV made it sound mildly interesting. But he said call back if we find there's some art missing and any sort of interstate trafficking of it. Until then he's not interested."

I scooped the last of the baba ghanoush with pita, chewed and swallowed. Finished the second beer. Leaned back. Sam finished the tabbouleh, put the napkin in front of her mouth and licked her teeth—the finely chopped parsley was notorious for getting stuck. She took a drink of water and surreptitiously swished it around her teeth before swallowing. Well, not so surreptitiously.

"Well, we know more now than we knew yesterday," I said.

"But we don't really know much."

"Not much."

"So what's the next step? Call GE and see if they're missing any trade secrets?"

"My gut tells me I wouldn't get very far with that line of questioning. I think I'll keep that in my hip pocket in case all the other trails go cold."

"All the other trails," she said.

"You have some parsley in your teeth."

"Damn! Thanks a bunch."

"You want me to not tell you?"

She took another drink, set the water glass down hard, swished and tried to force the water through the spaces in her teeth, didn't try to hide the fact, swallowed. Then she showed me her teeth.

"Gone," I said. I flashed a grin, ever so slight. She glared at me, but I'm pretty sure it was a mock glare.

"So, again," she said. "What's next?"

"Yeah, well. I guess I'll go see J.D. Fish this afternoon. Maybe visit Bobby G in the morning."

"Poke around. See if anyone gets nervous."

"That's the plan."
"Sounds like a brilliant plan."
"You think of anything better?"
"Absolutely not."

CHAPTER 10

The southeast part of Pleasant's gridded streets was the dustiest, grimiest. The streets were tidy by urban standards, but less so than the rest of Pleasant. It was light industrial mixed with wholesale: an iron worker, a place that dealt in stone, gravel and giant slabs of granite for countertops. Tucked in between those two businesses was a tiny space with an overhead garage door and no sign. I looked at the business card, compared it to the address numbers tacked above the door: 6496.

I rapped on the metal door. A minute later it swung up, the sounds of chains rattling. Cooler air rushed out of the dark space. Standing in the shadow was a man of average height, stocky but not fat, straight brown hair hanging halfway down his forehead and covering his ears. He wore a dirty, faded Arizona Cardinals baseball cap, a blue button-down work shirt, dirty white carpenter pants and yellow leather work boots.

"What can I do for you?" the man said, stepping into the sun.

"J.D. Fish?"

"Yep, in the flesh," the man said. "You want it, I build

it."

"Catchy slogan."

J.D. Fish didn't have an accent, exactly, but his speech was lazy, the way speech sometimes gets when someone spends a lifetime in a small town.

He smiled. "Thanks. I made it up myself. Kept me busy fifteen years now. Call me J.D." He extended a hand. I shook it.

"Eli Quinn," I said. "I'm looking into the murder of Tinker Bernstein. I was wondering if I could ask you a few questions."

A shadow crossed J.D. Fish's face.

"You a cop?"

"Private detective."

"Who hired you?"

"Delores Bernstein."

"How's she doing?"

"She's holding up pretty well," I said. "Wants to know who did this."

"I don't got any ideas. I guess you know I done some work for Tinker. Good man. I read about the murder. Hell, everybody knows about it. I called Delores, asked if I could do anything. She said no, thanks. That's all I know."

I looked around the shop space. Everything you would need to build a house with was in there: two-by-fours, roof tiles, metal flashing, windows of various sizes, a toilet. Stuff was stacked precariously high and, along the walls, on racks all the way to the ceiling. It looked like a dangerous place.

"That your only truck?" I pointed at a white Chevy with a ladder and some lumber strapped to the top of a rack, tool boxes mounted on each side. Big blue letters on the door said *J.D. Fish, Handyman. You want it, I build it.* The phone number inside the outline of a fish, address below.

"Yeah, just the one. Why? You think I had something to do with this? Hell, like I said, Tinker's a nice guy. He kept me busy, paid well. Why would I kill him?"

"I'm just asking questions, trying to figure out what happened. You've been there. You've seen all the art on his walls."

"Yeah, that crap? Tinker has a great house. But he's got lousy taste in art. Hell, some of that stuff doesn't even look like anything. Rest of it just looks old. All crap to me."

"What do you think of Delores Bernstein?"

"Don't know her very well. Tinker gimme the work, and he paid me. She always nice, though."

"When was the last time you were in the country club?"

"Look, buddy. I'm gonna give you the benefit of the doubt here, since you say Delores Bernstein hired you. But I got nothin' to hide, and I don't like you askin' me questions like I'm a criminal. If I had anything worth tellin' you, I'd tell you. But I don't. And I got a lot of work to do."

It was natural for someone who didn't do it to say they didn't do it when you hinted that he might've. It was also natural for someone who did it to say he didn't do it. In sum, I had nothing much to go on with J.D. Fish. I thanked him and left.

CHAPTER 11

The sky was on fire in the west, as a bank of puffy clouds hovered over the setting sun. It turned Pinnacle Peak and everything else, even the backyard, into an eerie but beautiful orange.

The air was still. There was a faint, distant hiss and rumble from the Loop 101, a short few miles away. Now and then the faraway throaty roar of a Harley dominated for a crackling moment. I heard a small jet taking off from Scottsdale airport.

With the mesquite charcoal firing up on the barbecue and some potato wedges in the oven, I pick a salad from the raised bed along the back fence. Spinach and chives, two medium-sized carrots, a ripe tomato.

Jeopardy was playing on the TV in the living room.

"Constantinople," I said to Alex Trebek's answer, "Istanbul." I never bothered to frame my response as a question. That gave me a split-second advantage over the contestants, one that didn't feel like cheating even though technically it probably was. "Easy one," I said.

I washed them, grated the carrots and sliced the tomato, put it all in another bowl. I ground some pepper into the salad and set it aside. I unwrapped two New York strip steaks that had been sitting on the counter an hour to get them to room temperature. I left one plain, sprinkled garlic salt and ground a lot of black pepper on both sides of the other. It was a total fallacy that you couldn't salt a steak before or during cooking. Whoever came up with that rule had never tasted one of mine.

Solo got up from his dog bed, turned a few circles, sniffed the air, laid back down.

I wished Sam were here. I didn't want to admit the wish, so I tried to concentrate on *Jeopardy* and on making dinner. The wish wouldn't go away.

Sam had caught me staring at her when she arrived at Café Amir for lunch. I expected it to feel wrong, because of Jess, but mostly it didn't. Mostly it felt good. The memory of Jess hovered over that moment, and returned now. It was a circle of emotions I was starting to think I might have to work through, eventually. Sam had been a friend so long, I was used to pushing aside thoughts of us being more than that. I was pretty good at pushing them aside, I was lousy at preventing them from coming. I wondered if maybe I should stop avoiding the feelings, if I could ever feel them without the heavy weight that followed them into my mind.

I opened a Guinness.

Flames were a foot above the charcoal chimney, loud sparks climbed several feet into the darkening sky. I dumped the charcoal into the barbecue, flattened the pile, then lowered the grill onto the charcoal and scraped it down. One key to a good steak was to superheat the grill surface. It went without saying that charcoal was better than gas. I did a number on the beer while I waited for the charcoal to settle in a bit. Then I raised the grill to about four inches off the charcoal and set the steaks on. I set the timer on my iPhone to four minutes.

I took the dirty plate back inside and rinsed it in the sink, finished the beer, and opened a bottle of Two Vines Merlot.

I sipped the wine and said "ottoman" to Alex Trebek, providing the question to an answer regarding home décor pairings. I dressed the salad simply, with olive oil and balsamic, and put it on the breakfast bar behind the sink. When the iPhone chimed I flipped the steaks and reset it for four minutes.

From the barbecue, I could see the TV. "The city in Ontario, Canada formed in 2001 by the combination of cities, towns and unincorporated areas around Sudbury," Trebek said.

"Who the hell would know that?" I asked out loud.

"What is Greater Sudbury?" said one of the contestants, a short, thin, severe woman from North Dakota who I had initially picked to finish second but who was now $4,200 ahead with Double Jeopardy nearly over. I cheered her on silently. The stuffy professor from Cornell who I'd figured to win was in second place, and the aerospace engineer from Pasadena had answered only three questions correctly, but lost all of his earnings with a wrong answer on a Daily Double.

I wondered if *Jeopardy* ever didn't exist, if Alex Trebek was doing the show on radio before television was born. I wondered how many other people in Pleasant were watching *Jeopardy* on this Friday night, and how many of them were pondering the radio angle. I wondered what Sam was doing.

I went back inside, turned the oven to broil to finish the potato wedges. Took a drink of wine.

My iPhone chimed again. I went back out, took the medium-rare steaks off the grill. I pulled the potatoes from the oven and scraped them into a bowl. I cut the unseasoned steak in half, carried it outside, slid one half into Solo's bowl. Solo had followed and sat near the bowl, quivering and looking at me. "Eat," I said. Solo lost all control.

I put the other half of Solo's steak into the fridge. Didn't bother to cover it. Jess would have put Saran Wrap over it. My eyes got wet. Didn't feel like succumbing, so I battled against the tears. Thought of Sam. That didn't feel right. Scratched the side of my head vigorously, trying to erase the thoughts, shifted my attention to the TV. I refilled the wine glass and sat down to eat and await Final Jeopardy.

CHAPTER 12

Much of Scottsdale was posh and expensive. Other areas were humble, with older, modest homes and tired suburban streets. Appearances suggested that Bobby Gonzalez—Bobby G as he liked to be called—had found a modest home that allowed him to live in one of the nation's more expensive zip codes without paying the high rent most people did. It was a 1950s tract model, squat and compact, nearly identical to the one on either side. Poorly tended palm trees lined the street, which was in need of repaving. Four-foot Cyclone fences surrounded most of the yards. A few had brown lawns. Most were gravel and cacti.

It was six o'clock Saturday morning. I picked the time because it was daylight but early, and I hoped to wake Bobby G without causing a stir in the neighborhood. And I knew from my reporting days, when you were asking tough questions, you wanted to catch people off guard. The more alert or prepared they were, the more effectively they could lie. Catch them drinking, sleeping, or otherwise unsuspecting, and you had a better chance of getting a raw reaction, a slip-up.

I parked the red Wrangler at the curb, in front of the

house, and hopped out. Solo sat in back, quivering with eagerness.

"Stay," I said. "But stay alert. If I need you, you'll know." I petted Solo's head and gave him a couple good slaps on the shoulder. If Solo had nodded in acknowledgement, I wouldn't have been surprised.

I went up the concrete walk. The front door was wood painted white, cracking and peeling near the bottom. There were three diamond-shaped windows of opaque, amber-colored glass at eye level. I knocked three times. Waited a minute. Nothing. There was a bell. I rang it, and I could hear it, an old-fashioned, two-tone chime. After another minute, a short, thin man in flannel pajama bottoms and a wife-beater shirt answered the door. He held it partway open with his left hand, so that only the right half of him was visible.

"The fuck," he said. "It's six in the morning. Who the hell are you?"

"Name's Eli Quinn. I want to ask you some questions about the Bernstein murder up in Pleasant."

Bobby G looked at me coldly. His eyes were nothing but black, the kind that don't look like they could ever contain or express warmth. Bobby G looked sleepy. His hair, long and black, was a mess. But he was suddenly awake and on guard, his eyes open a bit wider, the pupils dilated slightly. Solo growled, just enough to be heard. Bobby G looked over my shoulder at the dog.

"Don't know no fucking Bernstein," he said. He looked back at me. His eyelids had drooped a little. He looked sleepy again, or he looked like he was trying to look sleepy again. "What, you a cop?"

"Private detective."

"Then get the fuck off my property." He slammed the door.

I could've gotten a foot in the door. Could've forced my way in. Could've asked more questions. But that would have been risky. Bobby G wasn't known for shooting people, but that didn't mean there wasn't a gun on a table behind the door, or shoved into the back of his pajamas. Anyway, I'd done what I came to do. If Bobby G was involved, or if he knew who was, the hook had been set. I needed only wait and see what happened. If nothing happened, then maybe my impression was wrong and Bobby G wasn't involved. Maybe J.D. Fish was the killer. I still hadn't ruled out Delores Bernstein, or a possible Fish-Bernstein connection. And there were probably other possibilities. But if there was one common thread among bad guys, it was that they didn't like anyone stirring things up. So if you stirred, something usually happened, and it felt like I'd just stirred up a hornet's nest.

I walked back to the Jeep, told Solo he was a good boy, and drove off.

CHAPTER 13

I got back to Pleasant before seven a.m., nosed the Jeep into one of the diagonal parking slots in front of Lulu's Grind, next to a gaggle of Harleys all backed in neatly, two to a slot. The sun was behind the building, the air was warm and dry and the patio was all in shade. Outside, a few seniors, some alone and some couples, tied up most of the tables. I knew one couple and waved. A group of serious-looking cyclists in matching Spandex, already back from a morning ride, had pulled the remaining two tables together.

Inside, the Harley riders, none in Spandex, had all three booths against the wall. I didn't recognize any of them. There were three empty stools at the counter. Beach occupied the fourth. He was drinking coffee. I sat next to him.

"Hey, Beach. What you doing up so early on a Saturday?"

"You called me and said to meet you here. Otherwise I'd still be in bed, waiting for my honey bunch to wake up so I could try and get some nookie. Instead I'm down here competing for a seat. Someone's at my table outside. I guess those bicyclists don't know that's an official Sheriff's Posse member table."

"Those road bikers are tough guys. They probably knew and just wanted to push your buttons. Nookie?"

"You kids would call it something dirty."

Thankfully Lulu ended the conversational thread, coming out of the kitchen and pouring me a cup of coffee. "You early too," she said. "I thought you sleep in on Saturday."

"You know me, Lulu. I don't sleep that much."

"Maybe you need ta get out more," she said. "Find a girl finally. Have life again. Sex help you sleep, you know." She nodded her head up and down and wagged a finger side to side.

Beach laughed out loud. I gave Lulu a grin. Nobody ever said Lulu was shy. She was always giving advice, preaching optimism, move forward, live this life, you never know what tomorrow will bring so don't wait for it. Her attitudes were so stark, so refreshing, I wondered what shaped her—if her life in Tanzania had been really good or perhaps really terrible. I'd asked about her past a few times, but she always sidestepped the questions. "Tanzania is the past," she'd say. "My life here now."

"What you eat today?" she said.

"The usual," Beach said.

"Denver omelet?"

"Yup."

I asked, "Can I have the scrambled with sun-dried tomato?"

"You have anything you want," Lulu said. She smiled. I wondered if there was more meaning behind that comment than just breakfast. But I knew Lulu treated everyone special. I just thanked her and sipped my coffee. Enjoyed the place way too much to ruin it by trying to find out what Lulu really thought of me. Besides, she and Jess had been so close. They went to the gym together, jogged together, shopped together, and leaned on each other. I knew Jess had told Lulu about our fights, and probably also about the good things in our marriage. I figured Lulu probably knew more about me as a husband than anyone besides Jess. Used to bother me some, but now I found it somehow comforting. No way I could contemplate dating her. Not that I was ready to date. Not that she'd be interested. Anyway, there was Sam now, and I had to figure all that out. My head felt like eggs being scrambled.

Lulu left us to wait on the Harley riders.

"Beach," I said. "Need a favor."

"Glory hallelujah, I finally get to do something for *you*. What is it this time?"

"May have kicked a hornet's nest or two. Hoping you could keep an eye on Delores Bernstein. Just in case. Until I see what shakes out."

"Tell me about the hornet."

I told him about J.D. Fish, how he'd recently done a bunch of work on the Bernstein's house, and how I didn't think he was a hornet but anyway.

"Don't think Delores mentioned that to the deputies," Beach said.

"She said J.D.'s a nice guy, didn't occur to her to mention it."

"Hmmph. Well, I know of Fish. Don't know much about him."

"Run a background on him?"

"What, I'm your damn assistant now?"

I looked straight ahead, sipped my coffee.

"Will do."

Then I told him about Bobby G and the feeling I got this morning. Left out most of the detail on how I came to suspect Bobby G. Didn't want Beach to know about Sam's FBI connection. Didn't feel good about concealing information from my friend, especially since my friend was a posse member, and one who helped me with so much inside information. But it was how it was. Usually most people didn't need to know everything, sometimes didn't want to, and I was pretty good at deciding how much they needed to know.

"What made you suspect this Bobby G?" Beach asked, speaking quiet enough that nobody else could hear. He glanced over his shoulder, squeezing the red rubber ball with his left hand. He drank coffee with his right.

"If I tell you that, I'd have to kill you."

"Good luck with that, pardner. I'm still pretty quick at the draw."

"Let's just say I have a source."

Beach nodded, seemed OK with that. I was relieved.

"And you think Bobby G gonna go kill Delores Bernstein for the same reason he killed Tinker Bernstein.

"Don't know what Bobby G is going to do. Don't know who killed Bernstein. Don't know why. Don't know if Delores is in danger at all, or if maybe she's involved.

"That's a lot of things you don't know."

"Yeah, that's how this detective business works. It's how you know you have a case."

"By not knowing a lot of things."

"Exactly. Thing is, I just had a bad guy slam his door in my face, so I know he's not happy with me, and if I'm right, Bobby G—or someone—is going to make some noise."

"And you hope he does."

"Yep."

"Cause then you'll know who to suspect."

"Yep."

"You just might be a detective some day."

"Thanks, Beach."

The lawman glanced over his shoulder again.

"What are you looking for?"

"Nothing," he said. "I just don't like my back to the door. Any cowboy'll tell you not to sit with your back to the door.

"You afraid Doc Holliday gonna come backshoot you?"

"Or some Bobby G. There's always somebody out there

got shootin' on his mind, and a lawman's as good a target as any."

"That's why you always try to take the same table outside."

"Yep. With my back against the building, I can see the front door, see the street up and down."

"You crack me up, Beach. This ain't the Wild West anymore."

"It ain't? Whose house I gonna be watching day and night while you're out chasin' outlaws?"

"Touché. So you'll keep an eye on Delores?"

"We'll watch her house twenty-four-seven, follow her she goes anywhere. How 'bout you. You need backup?"

"I've got Solo."

"Solo got a gun?"

"Nope. Just big teeth."

"What about you?"

"My teeth aren't so big."

"A gun, I mean."

"Not gonna carry one."

"You should. The outlaws do."

"I'll manage."

"You can't karate-chop your way out of every tight spot. It almost got you killed last time."

"Taekwondo."

"Same thing," Beach said.

"Quite a bit different, actually."

"All the same at the end of a 9 millimeter."

"Got no choice," I said. "You know that."

"I know. You think the world would be safer if there were fewer guns. If people had to kill someone with their hands, they'd think twice."

"Or fail more when they do try," I said.

"And maybe if there were fewer guns, Jess would be alive," Beach said. We were both staring forward, at the orders up from the kitchen, under the heat lamps. "The world ain't perfect, Quinn. Not even in Pleasant."

"You'll watch Delores."

"Nobody gonna get near her."

"Thanks Beach. I owe you."

I put a twenty and a five on the counter, said goodbye to Lulu, and left.

CHAPTER 14

Fully breakfasted, I drove north up Pleasant Way. Pinnacle Peak loomed, centered by buildings on either side. The morning sun cast sharp shadows, making the mountain all lights and darks. I turned at the entrance to the country club and parked by the gate shack. It was just after eight o'clock.

I poked my head into the shack. A guard was sitting in a swivel chair, tapping on a keyboard, playing a computer game. Magazines were fanned on the desk, along with manila folders neatly stacked, a stapler, and the tablet computer they used to record license numbers. The guard was young, maybe twenty-three. Thin with pronounced, bony shoulders. A mop of curly brown hair. Not sure he knew I was standing there.

"What can I help you with?" he said, turning in his chair. His nametag said Martinson. He had a perpetual smile that showed large teeth. He stood up. He was lanky, maybe just under six feet tall, but looked taller than me at first glance. He had a slight stoop you'd expect from an older man.

"Eli Quinn." I stuck my hand out. Martinson shook it, not very firmly. "I'm looking into the murder of Tinker

Bernstein. Hoping you could help me understand a few things."

"My name's Mike. Mike Martinson. You a cop?"

Seems everyone was asking me that lately. I had decided to answer it honestly. Whenever that seemed like the best approach. "Private detective. Delores Bernstein hired me."

"All right, well. Mr. Bernstein. Yeah, he was a nice guy. Some of the country club people just drive through here, never look at me. Like they're too good to be seen talking to a security guard. Or maybe they're pissed to have to wait for me to open the gate that they wanted to live behind. Anyway, Mr. Bernstein always stopped to chat. Wife's real nice, too."

"What did you and Mr. Bernstein talk about?"

"Nothing in particular. He'd ask how I was. Ask about my son. My wife. He liked to tell me about his projects. I'm building a gaming computer, and he was helping me. He knows a lot about computers."

"I hear he was kind of a recluse."

Mike Martinson pondered a bit. "Well, now that you mention it, I don't know that much about him. Usually it was just him asking me about my life. He had a way of getting you into a conversation without ever getting around to talking about himself much. But when I told him I was building a computer, he got real interested. He gave me all kinds of advice, told me he used to work at GE. Engineer or something. Said he'd built several computers himself and actually built motherboards and other parts that go inside."

"Let me ask you something else," I said. "Could someone get in here without you knowing it?"

"Not unless they walked in, hopped a fence somewhere. This is the only place you can drive in, and we get every license plate number, take down a name, and if you aren't invited in by a guest or aren't on the contractor list, we don't let you through."

"I hear the camera was broken when Tinker Bernstein

was killed."

"You're not supposed to know that."

"I'm a detective. I know lots of stuff. I also know you're still taking plates manually, just as backup."

"Yep, that's right. But you didn't hear it from me."

I pretended to zip my lips. "So conceivably someone could come through, and if whoever was working the gate wanted to, they could just not write it down."

"We can't do that. Against policy."

"Right. And nobody would ever go against policy. You guys split what, three shifts daily?"

"Yep. It gets complicated with the rotations, but basically we're on four days, off three, so our days off don't always line up with the regular weekends. Kinda sucks, but we work less than forty hours a week and get paid like we were full-time, so that's not so bad."

"Can you tell me who was working the night Bernstein was killed?"

"I'm not supposed to."

"It's against policy."

"Totally."

"But can you?"

"Just a minute."

Martinson closed the shack door. I had to back off the threshold so it would close. He got on the phone, made a call. I hoped he wasn't calling his boss. People on the front lines of a company were often better sources of information than their bosses. I could see him and could hear that he was talking, but couldn't hear the words. Martinson hung up and opened the door.

"I called Delores Bernstein. She says you're who you say you are. She said the sheriff hasn't been able to solve the case, and you think you can. She says you're good at what you do, and that you're a good person. That all true?"

"I have a ton of flaws. But I suppose otherwise that's mostly true. I'm just trying to solve a murder, and the sheriff has pretty much stopped looking into it."

Mike Martinson looked at me a moment. Nodded a couple times. "I tell you, you don't tell anyone I told you."

"Scout's honor." I held up three fingers. Changed it to two. Wasn't sure.

"Let me look at the log just to make sure." He pulled a large binder off a shelf and thumbed through it. Pointed at the middle of one page. Yep, that's what I thought. "Earl was working that night, 3:30 p.m. to midnight."

"Earl have a last name?"

"Johnson."

Johnson. The gatemaster who'd stared at Sam.

"Heavy-set guy, pink-faced?"

"Yep, that's Earl."

"And what do you think of Earl Johnson?"

"Don't like him much. He comes off friendly when he wants to, you know? But he's the senior guy here, and he's on a power trip. Treats me like a kid. Treats visitors like they're lucky to get in under his watch."

"Yeah, I noticed. You think he's the honest, straight-up sort?"

"Eh, I don't know. Not sure what it is. Just a feeling. The guy kinda creeps me out, you know? I wouldn't trust him with something or someone I cared about, I guess."

I had run out of questions, so I looked around the guard shack, stalling. "That your magazine?" I pointed at the issue of *Make* sitting on the office desk.

"That's Earl's. He's a hobbyist. You know, drones, 3D printing, all that stuff. Kinda like Mr. Bernstein, only not as smart."

"They talk much?"

"Oh, yeah. Our shifts cross over by thirty minutes, gives us time to finish up paperwork or whatever, and one time I listened to Earl and Mr. Bernstein talk up a storm about 3D printing. Sounded like they'd discussed it before, picked up in the middle of a conversation, you know? Like I said, you get Mr. Bernstein going, he'd talk your leg off."

"Thanks Mike. You've been helpful."

"You think Earl Johnson killed him?"

"No, I don't. But things are starting to point in certain directions. For now, you could really help me if you don't mention our conversation to anyone."

"You think Earl was involved somehow."

"I don't know. But I can't rule it out. And until I know more, I'd rather he not know I know anything."

"You're being straightforward with me, but you're not telling me everything."

"Yep."

"And if I talk around, I put you and me in danger."

"You've been reading too many detective novels," I said. "But yes, that's possible."

"I'll keep it to myself. You need any more help, let me know. Mr. Bernstein was a good guy, you know? And none of us likes knowing there's a killer running loose in Pleasant."

"Thanks, Mike." We shook hands. I would've given Mike Martinson a business card, but I didn't have any yet. Made a mental note to get some made. Went back to the Jeep and drove off.

CHAPTER 15

With the ban on retail chain stores, there was no supermarket in Pleasant. There was a small grocery where you could buy milk and other basics, but the selections, particularly of fruits, vegetables and meats, weren't inspiring. Then there was the farmer's market on Saturdays, with great local produce seasonally. With all that, I left town about once a week for groceries.

I had two bags from Whole Foods down off Mayo Boulevard in Scottsdale. It was late and dark when I pulled onto Resolution Way. Across the street and half a block beyond my house was a small sedan, no lights on. A streetlight shone through the back window, so I could see the silhouette of a man sitting in the driver's seat. Since street parking wasn't allowed in the residential areas of Pleasant, you didn't have to be an Einstein to call the car suspicious. And you didn't have to be a Sherlock to deduce that the driver wasn't too bright—it would've been easy to not park near a streetlight.

I pulled into my driveway and stopped. I watched the sedan without looking at it. The headlights came on and I heard the engine start. The car moved quickly and swerved over to my side of the street, blocked the driveway. I pulled my iPhone from the holster, opened an app so it'd be ready, then I stepped out of the Jeep.

The driver got out and came toward me, not fast, not slow. He was taller than me, maybe six-three, with a ridiculously thick neck and weightlifter's arms bulging from a tight t-shirt. He had a large red scar that ran from the corner of his left eye to the corner of his mouth. His nose looked like it had been broken a time or two. A bulge in his right pants pocket looked suspiciously like a small gun.

"You Quinn?"

"I am. You the big guy with strong arms come to beat me up?"

"Don't fuck with me. I hear you been poking around in business of friend. I come to reason. You stop, I leave you alone. You don't stop, I break bones. I don't care which."

He had a thick Slavic accent of some sort.

"There's a third option," I said.

"Is no third option."

"I could not stop and you could not hurt me." I had the iPhone in my left hand. Both arms at my sides. My voice was casual. I wasn't one to taunt. Never let the opponent suspect what you're capable of. Reserve the element of surprise. My breathing was even, but I felt the blood pumping through me, felt my muscles tighten like coiled springs.

The Slav's eyes narrowed, his brow furrowed. Too many words to digest, apparently. "No third option," he said. "You been warned."

"Please tell me you're not going to hit me."

Predictably, the Slav came at me with a giant roundhouse right hand. I blocked it easily with my left, a high block in which my forearm redirected the punch off to the side. It was the simplest block in the business, and I was able to hang on to the phone. The brute's momentum carried him into my right fist, which came from belt high like a whip to meet his nose, which broke.

I jumped quickly backward. Never stay close to a big strong guy. Blood poured from the nose, and he spat some that had trickled into his mouth. If it had been the first time his nose were broken, the fight might've been over. But this guy seemed used to broken noses. He didn't even reach up to hold it. Instead he reached for his pocket. I used a quick sidekick to smash his hand against his hip. He grunted in pain but didn't back off. The gun stayed in the pocket.

I heard Solo bark once in the garage, having come through the doggie door from the house, as I knew he would.

The Slav moved in, more cautiously this time, with his hands up in classic boxing position. I pushed the button on the app to open the garage door, and a nanosecond later I jumped into the air and smacked the left side of the Slav's head with my right foot. The big guy was flat on his back just as Solo arrived. The dog dug his front paws into the Slav's chest, bared his teeth and growled, just loud enough to terrify any human being without alerting the neighbors. I reached around and removed the gun from his pocket. A .38 Special – not a big gun, but plenty effective at close range. Not the gun used in the crime, I knew. Caliber was wrong. He probably wasn't planning on killing me. Was sent just to break a bone or two. The gun was for just in case.

I used a detective line I'd learned on TV. "Who sent you?"

"Fuck you," he replied. Not a bad comeback. But he didn't sound as menacing as before, his voice up an octave now as Solo's teeth hovered a few inches above his nose.

I used the iPhone to snap a picture of his face.

"I think you're the one who's fucked right now," I said. "Tell me who sent you or I tell Solo here to go to the next phase of this drill."

"I don't squeal. Now get da damn dog off me. I go."

Primal brain signals told me, in an instant, that one more

kick could finish this guy. I could shoot him if I wanted to. I could unleash Solo. Those were the instinctual reactions you needed in a fight. But none of those scenarios would be pretty. And killing the Slav wouldn't help me figure out who killed Tinker Bernstein. As the rational thoughts supplanted the instinctual ones, my heart rate began to drop.

"Solo, heel," I said. He did. But he kept growling. I knew what I needed to know, and it would be to my advantage if whoever sent the Slav didn't know I knew who was behind it. Solo was a second slow in reacting, but he did as commanded. He backed up, sat next to me, put his teeth away, but kept a good growl going.

I pocketed the .38, then reached out a hand, helped the Slav to his feet.

"You used to box," I said.

"Fuck you. You broke nose. Finger, too, I think."

"Don't feel bad. You did your best. You OK to drive?" The immediate danger had passed. I'd won this round. No reason not to be civil. It was my tournament experience— you go a few rounds, then you bow, maybe bump fists, no hard feelings. I wondered if it was a healthy tactic in the present situation.

"Fuck you," the Slav said. He was a man of letters. Just not many. He headed to his car. As he opened the door, he said, "This not over." Solo growled some more. I just waved.

CHAPTER 16

Rubén González tinkled piano keys, from Cuba across time to Pandora through an iPhone into a crisp-sounding Bluetooth speaker half the size of a shoebox on the kitchen counter. Soup simmered, a creamed potato-spinach concoction I made up because all the recipes for creamed spinach included cream or corn starch. If you whipped potatoes in the blender with a little water, you could get the effect needed for a creamed soup base, and it'd be slightly less bad for you.

I tore arugula into pieces, dropped them into two salad bowls. Sliced a ripe pear thinly and added the slices to each bowl, then sprinkled some crumbled feta on top.

I opened a bottle of Horse Heaven Hills Merlot. Didn't know much about wine, but for the price, this was a really good one.

"This is robust, smoky. That work for you?"

"Those are the two qualities in wine I admire most," Sam said.

After the big Slav drove off and I'd put the groceries away, I called Sam to tell her what was going on. She insisted on coming over. I didn't resist. Some company would be good, and anyway, I wanted to tell her what I'd learned today.

I poured two glasses. Set one in front of her. She sat at the breakfast counter behind the sink, her back to the small living room and the large sliding doors at the back of the house. Solo sat next to her, his head leaning against her hip. She rubbed his head and I swear he smiled. It was late for dinner, but she said she hadn't eaten. I was beyond hungry.

I put a bowl of baba ghanoush and some pita in front of her. She scooped some and ate it.

"Not bad," she said. "This yours?"

"Made it earlier today. Eggplant is from the garden— first ones of the season. Here's the olive oil I was telling you about." I showed her a rectangular bottle. "It's fresh, dated. Makes all the difference in taste."

"I think Amir might still have a secret ingredient he's not telling you about, but this is very good."

Sam, always honest. I smiled.

I got the half a piece of steak out of the fridge from the night before and took it out back and dropped it into Solo's bowl. Solo waited for the command and devoured it.

"You feed him steak every night?"

"When I have one, he gets half of one. Then I give him the other half the next night. It's why he loves me."

"I thought you're not supposed to feed dogs real meat."

"Nothing wrong with real meat. Raw meat isn't a great idea. And bones can be bad. And they need more than just meat. He gets regular dog food every morning. But I think some meat is good for him. Keeps him strong, healthy and looking good."

"I think Solo is one of the best looking detectives I know," she said.

I raised an eyebrow theatrically.

"So start from the beginning," she said. "What did you learn about that contractor, Fish?"

"Nothing interesting, but he didn't seem particularly

evasive. Beach checked him out, says other than a couple traffic tickets and one drunk and disorderly, his record is clean."

"Doesn't mean he didn't do it."

"Nope. But he's not looking like a prime suspect."

"And what did you learn from Bobby G?"

"Not a lot."

"So he's not our guy?"

"I think he is."

Sam wrinkled her forehead, sipped her wine. I continued.

"I've seen it before. I told him I wanted to ask some questions about the Bernstein murder."

"You subtle devil you."

"That's me. Always a clever turn of phrase. So it's six a.m. and he's all sleepy. He got gruff, slammed the door. But I saw that thing I've seen before when you surprise someone, strike a nerve, and push them into a corner that forces a lie. His eyes got wide. Just for an instant. Only a trained detective would have seen it."

"Or an upstart private eye."

"Or one of those." I swirled the wine in my glass, to see if it had legs. I wasn't sure what exactly to look for, so I took a drink. The calming effect was surprisingly instant. I hadn't realized, but adrenaline had been coursing through me at an elevated level much of the day. I took a second drink, and consciously pulled my shoulders back and down a notch. "So I'm pretty sure things are stirred up. I asked Beach to watch Delores. If she's not the murderer, she could be in danger."

"Good call. Thank you."

I turned on the gas burner, put a small pan on and let it get hot. Poured in some olive oil, then added a handful of pine nuts to brown. I stirred them around. I got out two soup bowls, filled them, and put them on the counter.

"I don't think it's a coincidence that I piss off Bobby G this morning and the muscle is waiting for me tonight." I explained how the Slav had approached me, the clumsy punch, how I broke his nose, and how Solo put an end to the fight, while I got a jar out of the cupboard, measured in three tablespoons of olive oil, two of agave, two of balsamic vinegar, added a half teaspoon each of powdered ginger, salt and pepper. I screwed the lid on and shook it up. I left out the part about breaking a finger. I didn't want Sam to think *I* was the brute.

"So Solo saved your ass." Solo wagged his tail, done eating and happy to be part of the conversation.

"We're a good team. But this guy was all muscle, no brains. It wasn't much of a fight. I could have killed him easily."

"Listen to yourself, Quinn." She sat up straight, put her hands on her hips, mocked being very impressed.

I stood holding the jar of salad dressing. We locked eyes for a moment. I looked away first. "I didn't want to. Don't ever want to. But it's not like I've been jumped by a hoodlum before. I wasn't sure how it would all go down, but my mind took over. Everything was on autopilot. I guess being attacked kind of pissed me off." I drank some more wine. It was a good wine, and I recognized two or three distinct flavors as I swallowed. I didn't try to put names to them.

"I think that's an appropriate response," she said. "This isn't grade school where you're supposed to avoid a fight with a bully who punches you, otherwise they'll suspend you both. This is real life. A real bad guy. Eye for an eye, or something close to it."

"I had to stop myself though. My body was moving on to the next move, which would've put him in the hospital for a long time, at least, and my mind and body fought for an instant. Thing is, he's lying on the ground, defenseless. It was all just an instant, before Solo got there."

"And that scared you. Your potential."

"Not then. But later. When I called you, I noticed my

hands were shaking. That's only happened to me one other time."

"After you collared Jess' killer."

"And didn't kill him."

"But wanted to."

"Yeah, with him, I wanted to. Only thing that stopped me was I'd never been in a situation like that, and something nagged at the back of my mind, something I couldn't put a finger on, and I got confused, and so I didn't do it."

"But this time was different?"

I stirred the pine nuts as they browned. Had a sip of wine.

"Yeah. I didn't want to kill this guy." I told my story to the ceiling, to the dark wood cabinets, to the dark granite counters, to the travertine floor. I didn't look at Sam. "After I visited Bobby G this morning, I prepared myself mentally for the possibility that someone would try to scare me today or tomorrow. I thought about it, knew that to get to the bottom of all this, I needed to defend myself but not escalate the situation by killing someone."

"You kill somebody, the sheriff is back on the case, you're probably out."

"Right. Especially since I don't have a license. Not sure you know that, but you've pushed me into operating illegally."

"You can fix that."

"Yeah, I'll deal with it after this is over. So anyway, I knew I just needed to let them know I'm not a wimp. I ran scenarios through my head all day. Visualized. Prepared. Then when it actually happened, the instincts took over. It's amazing how calm I was. A bit like a machine. Afterward, thinking about that, it scared me."

"I think that's all normal. You've trained for this since you were a teenager. Your body knows what to do. Your muscle memory gets it done. But you're a good person, Quinn. You're not a killer."

"But I think I could be if I had to." I finished the glass of wine. Sam sipped hers. We looked at each other directly again.

"I think you could be too," she said. "It wasn't necessary this time. He struck first, and he got what he deserved. Solo helped. You got the gun away from him. Your self control kicked in."

I poured myself a second glass of wine. Sam's wasn't ready for a refill.

"Solo was right on the edge, too. I told him to back off and he did, but reluctantly. Otherwise he was mostly by the book. He got an A on responsiveness, and an A for position. A-plus on the baring of the teeth. But he flunked the bark. Only one, as usual. And like I said, he was a little slow to take his paws off the guy. I didn't mind that though. It was like his instincts and his self control had the same struggle for balance as mine."

"The Dynamic Duo."

"What are Batman and Robin?"

"Ha," Sam said. "You watched *Jeopardy* last night."

"Category: Famous Pairs." I had no idea Sam was a *Jeopardy* fan.

"We missed it tonight," she said.

"It was a busy night."

"And you and Solo did well."

I dressed the salads and put the salad bowls next to the soups. The pine nuts were browned. I spooned half of them onto each salad. The salad dressing sizzled. I put the pan in the sink, came around the counter and sat down next to her.

"Solo, in your place," I said. Solo went to his corner of the living room, curled up on his dog bed. "Eat the salad before the pine nuts cool," I said.

She forked a bite, careful to get some pine nuts and feta, a slice of pear and a bunch of arugula. "Jesus Christ," she said with her mouth still half full. "This is delicious."

"Maybe I should share the recipe with Amir," I said.

"Just leave something out," she said. "Payback." She took another bite. "Damn. Mmm."

I took out my iPhone, opened the camera app and showed Sam the picture of the Slav's face. "Look familiar?"

"Yeah, that's, um … Yuri. Yuri something. It'll come to me. Bouncer, muscleman, all-around tough guy. In and out of jail a few times. I ran across him when I was doing that series on the Ukrainian mob. They're not very organized here, but they make their share of trouble. Never seen him look scared like this, but that's definitely him."

"You recognized the scar."

"Yep, can't miss it. Is that Solo's muzzle?"

I looked at the photo again. A fuzzy brown patch in the lower right of the photo was out of focus. "Looks like it."

"Boiko," she said. "Yuri Boiko."

"He a shooter?"

"Not known for it. Mostly muscle. Shooters have to be smart, or they end up in jail for life. Boiko's not so smart, so he gets a lot of tough guy roles. If people back down, no shooter needed. He gets busted, he just says there was a misunderstanding, the other guy threw the first punch, we were arguing over a girl, whatever."

"That keeps him out of trouble?"

"Sometimes. Not always."

My wine glass was empty again. My salad was almost gone. I hadn't started on the soup. Sam had barely touched her wine. Or her food.

"Eat," I said. Solo's ears perked up. Sam ate. Solo dozed off. I poured myself another glass of wine. Hers was close enough to empty that I refilled it just so I wouldn't drain the bottle without sharing. We ate for a while in silence. It felt good to have Sam here, a foot away. The wine made me want to lean over, touch shoulders. I didn't dare. My right shoulder felt like a magnetic pole, and her left shoulder was the opposite, and if they touched, it would be really hard to pry them apart.

***

Sam rinsed the dishes and loaded the dishwasher while I lit the gas fireplace in the back yard. It was a warm evening, no need for a fire. But I liked the fire.

The slider was open and I walked back in. "Leave those," I said. "I've got more to tell you. And a theory."

Sam ignored me, finished loading the dishwasher. I opened another bottle, this an Argentinian Malbec—cheaper but good enough—and filled my glass. Hers wasn't empty so I took the bottle outside, sat down at one of the four cushioned iron chairs around the flagstone fireplace. Flames danced lazily on golf-ball-sized lava rock. Sam took the chair next to me. We were close enough to hold hands, but I steeled myself against that option. I was glad she sat next to me. I wouldn't have to make eye contact. We both looked at the fire.

"I had an interesting chat with one of the other guys who works the country club gate," I said. "Guy named Martinson. Nice kid. Seems straight up. Turns out he's a big fan of Tinker Bernstein, who was more talkative than Delores realizes. The kid—well, he's in his twenties, married, has a son—anyway, he's building a gaming computer and Bernstein's been giving him advice. Apparently if you got Bernstein talking about his passions, he opened up. So I asked him to look up who was working the gate the night of the murder. Earl Johnson."

"He's the pig we saw that day?"

"Filthy dirty. And very interested in you, as I recall."

"Or interested in parts of me."

The wine fed some responses into my brain. I suppressed them. "It didn't mean much until the kid tells me Earl Johnson and Tinker Bernstein were chatty, too. Earl's into 3D printing. Martinson overheard them discussing it one day."

"What's any of this got to do with art theft?"

"We've been thinking of art in terms of paintings," I said. "What about sculpture?"

"Sculpture and 3D printing."

"And a stolen PC."

"So what are you thinking? They stole some 3D printing files, plan to make copies and sell the fakes?"

"I don't know. I'm not sure there'd be a lot of money in sculpture replicas. And how would you sell a bunch of them without drawing attention to yourself? But it's one possibility, I guess."

"Is there another?"

I stared into the fire. Took another drink. "I don't know. But it's interesting that the PC was stolen, and Tinker Bernstein doesn't notice anything else missing, doesn't have any tips for the sheriff, doesn't seem nervous or distracted. Then three days later he's killed. What happened during those three days? What's the connection?"

We both watched the flames flicker gently. My eyes were getting heavy. I let them close.

"I better go," Sam said.

I opened my eyes. Wanted to stop her. Didn't try.

"You OK to drive?" I asked.

"I had less than a glass. You drank the rest. You OK to be alone?"

I searched the fire for an answer. Couldn't find one. Didn't look at her. Put my glass down. Pushed myself up.

"I'll walk you out."

CHAPTER 17

I woke up groggy from the wine. Sun bounced off ripples on the swimming pool and tossed frantic baubles of light on the ceiling through the bedroom window. I looked at the alarm clock, which said 8:27. I hadn't slept that late in weeks, maybe months.

I hauled myself out of bed, showered and brushed my teeth. I put on jeans and a gray t-shirt and my trail running shoes—loafers weren't the right shoes when you were fighting off bad guys. Breakfast was two eggs scrambled into some fried scallions and half a red bell pepper, finely chopped, with some cilantro thrown in at the last minute and a good amount of black pepper ground on top.

I had two cups of coffee before dialing the Franklin Institute in Philadelphia. I didn't know where else to start. I hoped to talk to a curator. After some runaround, I got through to Sally McKann, Senior Vice President, Programs, Marketing, & Business Development. I was surprised to get someone so high up on a Sunday.

"Sally McKann," she said. Not gruff, but businesslike.

I introduced myself, said I was a private detective, explained I was looking into the bust of Ben Franklin, the one done by the French sculptor Jean-Antoine Houdon back in 1778.

"Houdon," she said, correcting my pronunciation.

"Right," I said. "Not Houdini." Sally McKann didn't laugh. Thought she should have. Maybe she'd heard that one before. Or maybe she wasn't happy about working on a Sunday.

"I'm familiar with the bust," she said. "What's your interest in it?" Again, no charm, just business.

"Several questions, if you have just a few minutes. First, would replicas of the bust be worth much?"

"Mr. Quinn. We know this piece to be in a private collection. We don't know who or where. And I don't know you. Your questions raise suspicions. Why, exactly, do you want to know this information?"

"A man was killed," I said. "Caleb Bernstein. Tinker. He's known as Tinker. You can look the story up on AZCentral.com, the web site for *The Arizona Republic*."

She didn't say so, but I could hear some keys clack and figured she was looking up the story.

I continued. "Sheriff doesn't know why he was killed. Is calling it a random burglary gone bad. But Bernstein had a lot of art, and some sculptures, including the Franklin bust. You won't find mention of that in the story you're reading."

"You spying on me, Mr. Quinn?"

"I'm clever," I said, "but not omnipotent."

"Continue. I'm listening."

"Three days before he was killed, his place was broken into. They stole his PC, a TV, and apparently nothing else but a few tools. I have a hunch the TV and the tools were taken just to make it look like an ordinary theft. I'm thinking maybe there was something in the PC. This guy was a hobbyist, a maker, and he had a 3D scanner and a commercial-grade 3D printer. What if there were 3D files on that computer, which could be used to recreate the bust in perfect detail? I'm wondering if those would be worth anything."

"I'd have to ask a collector," she said. "But off the top of my head, I suppose the replicas would be worth something to someone. But that's not really art. It's like the posters you find in a shop down in the Village, or the prints of sunsets and seascapes at the mall. The fewer made, the more they'd be worth. But soon as someone did that, and assuming this is all black-market stuff, couldn't other people make copies of the copies?"

"I hadn't thought of that. Maybe you should be a detective."

Sally McKann laughed lightly. "I think I'll stick with my museum job."

"I understand the original is worth some three million dollars," I said. "That sound about right to you?"

"It does. In fact if we had the opportunity, we'd probably pay that. At auction, it might fetch more, but then we'd be forced to pass and the bust would be back in a private collection. That would be a shame, since almost no one would get to see it."

"Would it be difficult to sell the original?"

"Not particularly. Unfortunately, there is so much black-market trade in art, there are experts in the black market just like on the other side. If they vouch for it, there's no shortage of people with the means and the desire to own a piece like this."

"Could someone pass a fake off as real?" I asked.

"Not easy," she said. "I know they use a variety of materials in 3D printing, but I don't think marble is one of them. They might use paint or other media to try to make it look old, and look like marble. A good artist could probably do a good enough job to fool the average Joe. But any smart collector would instantly know it's fake. Plenty of black-market experts would be able to tell."

"How would one tell?" I asked.

"First, the weight. Marble is heavy. Maybe a fake would

weigh the same, but that would be the quickest way to tell. Second, marble tends to turn yellowish or brownish as it ages. Over the centuries, whenever a piece is handled, skin oil can rub off and cause this. A fake might be abnormally white. Finally, marble has natural imperfections. I would imagine a 3D-printed copy would be homogenous in tone and color. If someone tried to add imperfections, probably even I could tell by looking closely."

"If I texted you a photo of a sculpture, would you be able to tell if it were real or fake?"

"Maybe," she said.

Without having to rely on any charm, I got Sally McKann's cell phone number so I could text her photos of the bust.

CHAPTER 18

Mike Martinson was working the gate to country club. I stopped and said hello when he came out of the guard shack, his big teeth on display as always, shoulders hunched slightly. Solo was watchful, but didn't growl.

"Solve the case yet?"

"Not yet, but I've learned some things that point in a very interesting direction. I'm heading up to see Delores Bernstein now, hopefully confirm something."

"You think Earl Johnson did it?"

"Let's just say you should continue to lay low, not speak about our conversation," I said. "Earl still coming to work each day?"

"Yes. He was on the overnight the past couple nights."

"Thanks. Can you let me in?"

"Sure. I'll just get your license number and write it down, you know?" He did. Then he opened the gate. "Good luck," he said.

***

I waved to Bill Henshaw, who was parked at the curb in front of the Bernstein house in one of the posse cars—they looked virtually identical to sheriff cars. Beach had posted someone, as promised. Henshaw waved back. I hit the buzzer and Delores let me in.

"Good morning, Delores. How are you?"

"Except for having a sheriff deputy parked out there all day and night, and following me everywhere I go, I'm fine."

"It's for your own good." I explained what was going on. She said she understood. "I'm hoping we can put an end to all this soon. I'd like to see the Franklin bust."

Despite the rising heat outside, the house was freezing. She wore a tan cashmere sweater and sharply creased tan slacks. She showed me to the bust.

I asked, "Have you ever looked closely at this thing?"

"Not really. I like some of the paintings, mostly the newer, more modern ones, but sculpture has never really interested me much. And I don't care for busts at all. There's something kind of creepy about them. The eyes, frozen in time, staring out, the chopped off shoulders. I don't know. Maybe it's just me."

"I'm not overly fond of busts myself." I looked closely at Ben Franklin. Asked her to. "Does it look real to you?"

"Do you think it's not real? Tinker paid ..."

"I think the real one might've been stolen the night Tinker was killed," I said. "If I'm right, this one was made on a 3D printer, using a file from Tinker's computer. That's why they stole the computer, I'm thinking. And that would explain why he was killed three days later. They came back, shot him, swapped the fake bust for the real one, and now they're trying to sell the real one. They probably figured Tinker would've noticed right away, but they were counting on nobody else noticing, at least for a while. That'd buy them some time to get rich, maybe leave the country, before anyone knew there'd been a theft."

"You're sure about all this," she said.

"Not at all. It's just a working theory."

"What other theories do you have?"

"None. But I may be able to find out pretty quickly if this one's fake." I used my iPhone to take three photos of the bust: overview, medium and tight—just like photojournalists were trained to do. Texted them to Sally McKann at the Franklin Institute, waited a couple minutes, then called her.

"I'm looking at them," she said when she answered. "The photos aren't very good."

"I'm a detective, used to be a journalist. Spent some time on Wall Street. I'm definitely *not* a photographer."

"Still, the pictures took my breath away. I haven't seen this bust since it was last auctioned off. A beautiful piece. Can't tell what the second photo is supposed to show."

"Medium shot. It's a technique."

"Well, it's useless. Let me look at the third one."

I looked at the area of the bust I'd used for the third photo. It had some discoloration, darker than the surrounding area, and I'd picked it so she could see an area that had been worked on, if it were indeed fake.

"You see that browner area," she said. "That doesn't look natural to me. But it's hard to tell in this photo. I can't be sure."

I asked, "How much should this thing weigh?"

"I don't know exactly, probably eighty pounds or more. It would not be easy to lift. And in fact it should be secured to the pedestal anyway. If it's the real thing, the collector would have made sure it was secure."

"Hang on." I set the phone down on the coffee table. To Delores I said, "Mind if I try to pick it up?"

"Oh my. Be careful. But yes, go ahead."

I lifted the bust right off the pedestal. It was heavy, but nowhere near eighty pounds. Maybe thirty or forty.

"The good news," I said to Sally McKann, "is you've helped me figure this case out."

"I'm guessing that the bad news is Houdon's Franklin bust is missing for the second time," Sally McKann said.

"If I find it, I'll call you. I think you might be interested in speaking with the rightful owner."

CHAPTER 19

I had met Jess in New York, while I was working in the Financial District. She was in banking, but to her it was a job, not a career. We married just before I quit Wall Street, and she paid the bills while I went back to school. She had no family there, and she was excited to move to Arizona when I got the newspaper job. We had lived modestly, happily at first, and we'd talked about starting a family. She found another bank job, but it was less interesting to her than before. We started having fights. Nothing major, but if good relationships can be compared to spring and summer, ours was starting to feel like autumn. Her family was in Nebraska, and she began hinting that we might be better off there. I wasn't very interested in Nebraska. We'd had a fight about that the evening before she was killed, and we didn't say goodbye to each other that morning.

That's what I was thinking about as I backed Jess' Jeep Grand Cherokee out of the garage. The Cherokee hadn't been used since she was killed. I'd never needed it, but I hadn't gotten around to selling it. I ran it every few weeks to make sure the battery was charged. Today I needed it. Being a white SUV, it looked like half the vehicles on the road in and around Scottsdale. I was headed back to Bobby G's house, and I didn't want Bobby G to notice me. The red Wrangler wouldn't provide very good cover.

Solo was in the back, curled up. Without the wind in his face, there was nothing to do but curl up.

Traffic was light on the 101 Southbound, and I made good time to the Thomas Road exit, went right. Between Hayden and Scottsdale Road I turned right again, then took a left onto Bobby G's street. Pulled to the curb a block away, behind another car and in front of a vacant lot.

It was just past noon. I had a chicken-hummus wrap from Amir's Café, a banana, two granola bars and two bottles of water. I rolled the windows down, turned off the engine. The light breeze kept me reasonably comfortable. I put a Jason Mraz station on Pandora, bluetoothed it to the Jeep's stereo, volume low. I unwrapped the wrap and took a bite, and settled in to wait. The wrap, lemon and garlic the dominant flavors, was amazing.

I had no idea if Bobby G was home. And I still didn't know who had done what, or even for sure who was involved. I had three suspects on my most-likely list, but hadn't connected any of them to each other. Only Yuri Boiko was a sure bet, but I didn't figure Boiko for the brains. I couldn't think of any way to move the investigation forward, and since Bobby G was the one I most strongly suspected of being the mastermind, he seemed the best bet to tail. Plus I knew where Bobby G lived.

At exactly three o'clock, nothing had happened. By four p.m. I was wondering if I was wasting my time. For all I knew Bobby G was in the Bahamas by now, counting his money. But I didn't have anything else pressing to do, so I ate the banana and practiced sitting some more. I'd done a few stakeouts as an investigative journalist, and there was only one skill required: patience. It was something I had lots of, so I decided to use some more. In fact, I was rather enjoying myself despite the boredom. I was doing something. OK, it was actually just sitting, and thinking, but at least it was all for a good reason.

I got out and took Solo over to the vacant lot so we could both do what guys need to do when they've been in a car for four hours. After he peed on two small, scraggly bushes, one large rock and a signpost, Solo communicated a desire to play fetch, but I asked him to get back in the Cherokee, and he complied.

At a little past five o'clock, a black Mustang pulled into the driveway. I was too far away to be noticed, but I slouched down some anyway. Bobby G got out, looking a little more dapper than the last time I had seen him. He wore a gray pinstripe suit with a vest, gold in the back, and polished black shoes. He draped a sport jacket over his arm, shut the car door, and went in the house.

If Bobby G were home for the night, he'd probably have put the Mustang in the garage. So I had a granola bar and waited some more. A little past seven, the sun went down. I ate the last granola bar and finished the water. A few minutes later Bobby G came out, dressed the same but with his jacket on. He got in his Mustang, put the top down, and drove off. Lucky for me, the Mustang went in the opposite direction. A lot easier to tail someone without being noticed if they don't drive right past you first.

I started the Cherokee, pulled onto the street casually, left the lights off. The black Mustang made a couple of right turns, and I let him stay just more than a block ahead. Bobby G had his lights on. The characteristic three vertical bars on each taillight made Mustangs about the easiest cars to tail. The taillights turned left onto Thomas, a four-lane boulevard that was busy. Dusk was turning quickly to night. I turned my headlights on before I turned onto Thomas, stayed about a block behind the Mustang, always making sure there were a couple cars between us.

As Bobby G's taillights approached the 101, I backed

off. From two blocks back, I'd be able to tell if he went North or South or straight, and it'd be easy to get back on his tail. The taillights went north. I lost him for about twenty seconds, then sped up and found the taillights before the next off-ramp. I slowed down to match the Mustang's speed and stayed well back.

The Mustang kept up with traffic, which was mostly moving at about ten miles an hour over the speed limit. I kept the same pace, changed lanes only when I needed to. Tailing at night wasn't hard. Just don't get too close, don't drive like an idiot. Unless the other guy expected someone would be tailing him, he had no reason to suspect you or any of the other six or so cars between you and him.

Bobby G's Mustang pulled off on Pima Road and continued North toward Pinnacle Peak and Pleasant. There were fewer cars on this six-lane boulevard, but it was fully dark now. I left two cars between us. After a few minutes, the Mustang turned right into a small subdivision called Desert Rose. There was no gate, but the homes were large, probably half a million and up.

When the Mustang took a left onto a narrower street, I waited. There was no traffic, risky to follow too closely. I turned the headlights off, then sped up and took the left, on Roadrunner Lane, just in time to see the Mustang go right two blocks later. I slowed again, then pulled ahead. The turn was Drinkwater Court, and I kept going. It was a dead-end with a cul-de-sac, so I waited a minute, until I figured Bobby G would be inside whatever house he was visiting, then I turned around and parked on the other side of Roadrunner Lane. I got out and walked into Drinkwater Court. There were five houses on the cul-de-sac. The black Mustang was parked in front of 3434. I went back to the Cherokee and called Jack Beachum.

"Beach, need a favor. You near a computer?"

"Sure, Quinn. I'm sitting here surfing porn with my wife. Been hoping you'd call so I could do you a favor."

"You're at the substation, aren't you?"

"I am. And I have reports to fill out, all on paper, and a posse scanner to listen to, and a book to read if I get bored, but there's a computer sitting here that I can use if I must."

"Need you to look up 3434 Drinkwater Court. Might be North Scottsdale, might be unincorporated, not sure. Just north of the 101 off Pima. Tell me who lives there."

"What's going on?"

"I tailed Bobby G, this is where he is. Need to know who he's visiting."

"You know I'm not supposed to be working crimes," Beach said. "I'm just the phone answerer who gets to drive an official-looking sheriff car, then call in backup if anything actually happens."

"C'mon, Beach. We break this case you'll be captain soon."

"We?"

"Please?"

"Earl Johnson."

"No shit?"

"As God is my witness, says so here, in the official posse computer. Works for Dribbs Security."

"Earl Johnson's the owner of the house?"

"Says so here."

"Hot damn," I said. "I think we just cracked this case. Earl Johnson makes, what do you figure, maybe twenty-five, thirty-k as a gate guard for Dribbs?"

"Forty tops."

"And he owns a house worth at least half a mil, be my guess. What else can you tell me about Earl Johnson?"

"Was a cop in Tempe. Fired."

"For?"

"If I'm not careful, *I'm* gonna get fired. Be careful with this information."

"You know I will be."

"Let's just say he was fired for suspicious activity."

"Hey Beach, you ever heard of a cop getting fired for, say, theft?"

"Ha, that's a good one. I suppose it's happened before."

"I wonder if that's what happened to Earl Johnson," I said.

Beach didn't say anything.

"Thanks, Beach. I owe you one."

"I probably wouldn't say no to a glass of Dewar's in a back yard around a fire pit."

"I'll send you an invite soon as I wrap this up."

.

CHAPTER 20

A few minutes after I hung up with Beach, the black Mustang pulled out of Drinkwater Court and turned left on Roadrunner. There was only one way out of the small subdivision, so I waited and let Bobby G get a good head start. I caught sight of the Mustang's taillights again just as it turned south on Pima Road. I followed the taillights at a good distance until they turned into a strip mall and parked in front of Cactus Joe's Bar & Grill.

The strip mall was the usual, Spanish architecture housing a Cameo Cleaners, a Pizza Hut, a Walgreens and a half-dozen other establishments. Palo verde trees sprang from the parking lot.

I parked on the opposite side of the lot, nearest the road, and several spots down. I watched Bobby G walk into Cactus Joe's. It was mostly bar, not so much grill. A place where men walked in, and women walked in, and men and women walked out together. Nobody ever complimented the food, but there were interesting rumors about after-hours parties that involved lots of different substances, dancing on the bar, and not much clothing.

I dialed Sam.

"Can you tail someone for me?"

"Do you mean *am I capable* or *am I willing?*"

"Yes."

"I'm going to pretend you wouldn't actually ask the first question, because that would be either sexist or a display of your ignorance about me, or both. So I'll take the second question. Sure. What else would I want to do on a Sunday night?"

"I'm at Cactus Joe's off Pima, just north of the 101. You know it?"

"Can't say I've been there, but I know where it is. The pickup joint, right?"

"Yep."

"And you're there because…"

"Bobby G just went inside. I need you to sit on him, follow if he goes anywhere. How soon can you be here?"

"Ten minutes."

"Park next to me, south end of the lot. I'm in Jess' Cherokee."

***

Sam pulled into the parking lot thirteen minutes later. I got out and went around to her driver's side. She rolled the window down.

"You're late," I said.

"Had to change," she said.

She was wearing jeans and a t-shirt. I smelled a perfume I'd never smelled before, wondered if maybe she was out with someone. None of my business. And Jesus, Quinn, you're chasing a likely killer. You're on the clock. Get your head in the game.

"Hello?" Sam said.

I realized I was staring at her again. I looked up over the hood of her car toward the bar. "Things came together today," I said.

"What happened?"

"I detected."

"Which means?"

"I made a phone call. Then I sat in my car for seven hours."

"Tell me."

I watched two older men go into Cactus Joe's. Nobody came out.

"You remember the bust of Ben Franklin at the Bernstein's," I said. "It's a fake."

"You're shitting me."

"I wouldn't. It was made on a 3D printer. That's the file that was on Tinker's computer. At least that's my theory, and it's looking pretty solid right now."

"So there was an art theft, just nobody knew it."

"Right. They made the fake, came back three days later and swapped it for the real one, killed Bernstein because he's the only person who would've noticed the fake right away."

"And Delores was out when that happened," she said. "You have to wonder if they knew she was out."

"You do. And you have to wonder how they got into a gated community, stole an eighty-pound bust, and nobody saw them come or go."

"Not so practical to hop a fence with a heavy, three-million dollar, 280-year-old bust," she said.

"Easier to just drive out."

"And they had a record of everyone who went in and out," she said. "So it's likely someone on that list."

"I don't think so. I went back to Bobby G's house, spent the day watching it just sit there. He comes home around five. Drives that black Mustang over there." I pointed to the car, sitting near the entrance to Cactus Joe's. "Couple hours later he heads out. I follow him to a small subdivision just north of here, Desert Rose, about halfway between here and Pleasant."

"I know it. Small, no gate, but nice homes. They cleared the lots before the recession, built two or three places, then it sat a few years. They started construction again a couple years ago and just recently finished the last homes."

"Turns out Bobby G is visiting Earl Johnson."

"The gate guard with the crush on me. Darn, it's looking like I'm going to have to give up my dream to date that man."

"Yeah, you'd have made a nice couple."

"So you're thinking Earl Johnson lets Bobby G know the Bernsteins are away the first night, then lets him slip in and steal the PC. Then gives him a free pass again three nights later."

"I'm headed to his place now, and I have a hunch me and your dream date aren't going to get along very well."

Sam's face scrunched with a puzzled look. "How did they even know about the bust in the first place?"

"Not sure. But remember Mike Martinson, the other gate guard, said Earl Johnson was chatty with Tinker Bernstein. I figure Tinker may have mentioned the bust, said he had made a 3D scan of it, something like that. It's a hole I haven't plugged. But everything else feels pretty tight. If I can find the bust, the details will fill themselves in."

"What do you want me to do?"

She looked up at me in a way I'd noticed before, her head tilted to one side, her eyes looking up. Oh, man, it was hard to just have a conversation with this woman. Like in some black and white movie, she batted her eyes. Actually she just blinked and I saw what I wanted to see. Is that what I wanted to see? Jesus, I did want to see it. Well, maybe not actual eye-batting, but something that would tell me we might be moving into a new phase of our relationship. My way of thinking about Sam had changed these past four days. My next thought was of Jess, and my mind became a swirl of confusion again.

"Quinn?"

I'd done the staring thing again.

"Sorry, thinking."

"You've been doing that a lot lately. I hope it doesn't hurt."

"Not at all." Well, maybe a little. But it felt good, too. Really good. "Anyway, just tail Bobby G. If I'm right about all this, he's at the center of it. He might have the bust, but I don't think so. He's too smart for that. I'll go visit Earl Johnson, see if I can squeeze some more information out of this case. Maybe he has the bust."

"Earl Johnson will be easier to squeeze than Bobby G."

"Exactly. Bobby G is slippery. Earl Johnson is closer to stupid. I'll call you when I figure out the next move. So just keep tabs on Bobby G." I looked at the bar. A young woman came out with a middle-aged man. Bobby G's car still sat there. "Mustangs are easy to tail," I said.

"Have been since 1965," she said. "The taillights."

"Sixty four and a half," I said.

"Ah, right. Well, I was always more of a Camaro girl."

I bent down, put my hands on the top of the door. Sniffed a bit. "What's that smell?" I said.

"What smell?"

"Perfume" I said. "I didn't know you used perfume."

She gripped the steering wheel tightly, looked straight ahead. "I'm a girl, Quinn. There are many things you don't know about me."

"So, were you on a date with Earl when I called?"

She blew a bunch of air out her nose and laughed. "None of your business what I was doing when you called. And speaking of business…"

I stood up to leave, looked at the door of the bar again. Then I said, "Well, I like it." I turned to go.

"Quinn?" I stopped but didn't turn around. I was afraid I might not walk away if I did. "Please be careful," she said. "I'd like to see you in one piece again."

I smiled to myself, nodded, and headed to the Cherokee.

CHAPTER 21

The lights were on downstairs at 3434 Drinkwater Court. I parked out on Roadrunner and walked into the poorly lit cul-de-sac so Earl Johnson wouldn't get a heads-up he was being visited. I left Solo in the Cherokee. I didn't think Earl Johnson would present much of a problem, and if Earl spotted someone with a German shepherd coming up the sidewalk, he'd more easily figure out it was me.

The changing scenes of a TV show flashed lighter and darker in a front window. I rang the doorbell. The volume on the TV went down. A few seconds later Earl opened the door halfway. He was in dark blue sweat pants and a white t-shirt that left a couple inches of his well-fed belly exposed. A stain on the shirt suggested pizza was for dinner. His pink face was redder now, probably a few beers into the night.

I kicked the door, a swift but not-so-subtle act that smashed Earl Johnson in the face and sent him flying back faster than his chubby Boss Hogg legs could carry him. He fell on his ass. A small revolver skittered out of his hand and across the floor. I moved in quickly and carefully picked the gun up with the tips of my thumb and forefinger and put it on an entry table. I didn't know much about this part of the job, but I knew enough to be careful about the evidence. The gun had Earl Johnson's greasy fingerprints on it, and I didn't want to mess that up.

"What the hell," Earl said, scrambling like a walrus to get off the floor. His eyes were watered—apparently I'd broken another nose—and his vision would be blurred. "Who the fuck…"

"Hi Earl. Eli Quinn. We met at your gate the other day. My dog didn't like you. I didn't like you. Sam Marcos doesn't like you. And now I find out you're not just a disgusting pig of a man, but also a thief."

"The fuck you talking about, asshole." He cupped his nose with his hands. I knew several ways to disable a man. Among the simplest was to break his nose. It was a big target, breaking it didn't cause any life-threatening damage, and it was nearly impossible to continue fighting with a broken nose and blurry eyes. Unless you're Yuri Boiko. Earl Johnson was no Yuri Boiko. Earl had lost the whole fight in Round 1, even if he hadn't admitted defeat yet.

"What'd you pay for this place, Earl? Half a million? Briggs Security paying you pretty well I guess. Either that, or this thieving thing is a habit. I know what happened in Mesa. But now you've gone and killed somebody. Bye-bye fancy home. Hello Big House."

Earl was on one knee now. He glanced at the revolver. He looked down at the floor. Plotting. I was the third point of an isosceles triangle in the favorable geometry of the situation, equidistant between Earl and the gun.

Without looking up, Earl said, "Listen, Buster, you better get the fuck out of here right now, or else you're a dead man."

"Buster? Nobody's called me Buster since I was a kid. But thanks for the segue. I've been meaning to ask you, Earl. Where's the Franklin bust?"

Earl Johnson made a pathetically slow dash for the

revolver. That was the move I was looking for. No doubt left that Earl Johnson was in on the crime. He didn't even try to deny it.

Interesting how much can flash through your mind when you know violence is coming. Here's what occurred to me in that instant: Over the past four days, I had grown fond of Delores Bernstein and, by extension, Tinker Bernstein. Tinker's death was senseless. Two lives ruined. There was no telling what would happen to Earl Johnson in the courts. And while I didn't want to become a vigilante, I could not shake the anger of Jess' killer getting off for anything less than a death sentence. You might think you're against the death sentence until someone kills someone you love. Deep inside I'm still against it, but in that case, part of me wanted it. But that was in the past now. I had Earl Johnson to deal with. I could simply shove him to the ground again, grab the gun, and call 9-1-1. I didn't. Earl had barely gotten to his feet and lunged halfway toward the gun when I grabbed his left wrist with my left hand, used my right forearm to break his left elbow as his momentum was redirected to the floor. His broken nose slammed into the floor and left a bloody mess on the tile. He screamed like a six-year-old girl. The scream was probably for the elbow, which would hurt way more than the nose.

My breathing was elevated more than it should have been. I was crouched in the ready position, both fists balled at my belt, left foot slightly forward. I blinked. Earl Johnson rolled over onto his back, put his right hand up to signal *no more*. His left arm lay on the floor at an impossible angle. I wasn't squeamish, but the sight of the helpless man recalibrated my brain. I took a deep breath and stood up straight, extended my fingers to stretch my hands, made the muscles in my neck and shoulders relax. The tension eased downward from there.

I grabbed Earl Johnson by the collar with one hand, put my other arm under his right armpit and lifted him to his feet. He groaned in pain.

"Let's have a look around, Earl." I pushed him into the hallway.

"Listen. I don't know what you're talking about."

"Earl. Stop fucking with me. You killed Tinker Bernstein, stole his bust of Ben Franklin, replaced it with a 3D-printed fake." I was pretty sure Earl Johnson hadn't actually done any of those things himself. He probably made the replica, fudged Delores Bernstein's time of entry through the gate the night her husband was killed. Then tipped the thief and killer—probably Bobby G and Boiko— when to get in. Then tipped them just as Delores came back, when to shoot the clock, which Bobby G would have set ahead first. The details didn't matter right now. The accusations would give Earl something to truthfully deny, thereby further admitting his involvement in the whole thing. I enjoyed mind games, and I'd be really disappointed to lose one with Earl Johnson. I pushed him from door to door down the hallway, kicking each door in. I didn't need to kick the doors in, but they were cheap, hollow doors, easy to kick in, and they made a lot of noise when I did so. The effect seemed scary. So I kept doing it.

"I didn't kill Bernstein," he said. "I didn't steal nothing."

"Yuri Boiko do the killing?"

Earl didn't reply. I read his speechlessness as a yes.

"Bobby G do the stealing?"

Again, no reply.

"Where's the bust, Earl? I know you know where it is. Too risky to store it at Bobby G's, since he's a known art thief. Boiko's too stupid to leave it with him. You're not as stupid as Boiko, but you're stupider than Bobby G, so I'll bet three million dollars the bust is here."

Earl didn't say anything. I opened the garage door. Garage doors are solid, to help prevent the spread of fire from the garage to the house. Trying to kick one in would just be dumb. Pushed Earl through it. In the middle of the room was a commercial-grade 3D printer.

"Bingo," I said. "Tell me where the bust is, Earl, or I'm going to break your other elbow and you won't be able to wipe your own ass while you're in jail. I'm sure there's some dudes there love to do it for you."

Earl Johnson hung his head. He had the look of someone who'd been defeated many times in life. Without him noticing, I flicked on the recorder of my iPhone. I stayed behind Earl, holding him by the collar. "Where's the Franklin bust, Earl?"

"Master bedroom," Earl said, his voice low and dejected, his speech laced with pain. "In the closet behind the shoe rack." I turned the recorder off so it wouldn't record Earl's moaning. The pain had likely gone from sharp to dull and searing, the sort of pain that causes a man to black out.

I pushed him back through the hall, into the living room and over to the entryway. Turned the recorder back on.

"You kill Tinker Bernstein?"

"I need some aspirin. A doctor. Fucking hurts, man."

Recorder off. I'd erase that one. "I agree," I said. "You need something to kill the pain, and you need a doctor. I'll call somebody soon as you answer me. Or we can sit here and talk all night." Recorder back on. "You kill Tinker Bernstein?"

Earl closed his eyes. The pain was beyond bearable. The man was getting woozy. "Boiko done that," he said.

"And you stole Bernstein's PC, printed the fake, swapped it for the real one while Boiko shot Bernstein."

"I didn't steal nothing," he said.

"Who did the theft?"

"Was Bobby G."

Recorder off. Then Earl Johnson's eyes rolled back in his head. I caught him as he fainted and laid him gently on tile, same spot he'd gone down before.

.

CHAPTER 22

"He's been out cold since I called you. But he's breathing fine."

"What happened to his nose?" Beach asked.

"There was some disagreement whether I'd been invited into his home or not," I explained. "The door sort of settled things for us."

"What happened to his elbow?"

"Somehow his gun ended up on the table over there." I pointed at the revolver near the front door. "After his run-in with the door, he went for the gun. I didn't think it would be good for him to have the gun, so I kind of got in the way, and I guess he fell. Things happened fast. I feel terrible. It was all a big misunderstanding."

Beach chuckled. He fingered the gun, put it in a plastic bag, and zipped it shut.

"I thought you posse guys don't do crime scene work."

"Can't have a suspect waking up and shooting us. I think the boss man will understand."

Beach pulled out plastic handcuffs and zipped Earl Johnson's ankles together. I led my friend into the master bedroom, pulled the shoe rack out and we found the Franklin bust, which neither of us touched. Evidence.

"Three million bucks," Beach said.

"Good a reason to kill an innocent man as any," I said. We went down the hall and into the garage. I pointed at the machine. "He made the fake there, I'll bet. You'll probably find some raw material— the *ink*, as it were—to match the replica. The ink is not marble, by the way. Weighs about half as much, whatever it is. I don't see Tinker Bernstein's PC, but I bet you'll find the 3D file of the Franklin bust on that laptop." I pointed. "That'll be what you posse members call evidence. PC is probably in a dumpster somewhere." We walked back through the hall, across the living room to the entryway.

"And you want me to fix all this with the sheriff, make sure you don't go to jail for beating this guy up, make sure the evidence isn't screwed up, make sure the case is tight."

"That was the idea. And if you could do me a favor, I'd like to come out of all this with a Detective Agency license."

"Yeah, I surely owe you a favor." Beach shook his head. He took a deep breath, looked down at Earl Johnson. "Your first case."

I nodded. Felt something stir inside me. It wasn't happiness. It wasn't the thrill of victory. It definitely wasn't what I'd done to Earl Johnson, which simply struck me as unpleasant but necessary. What was it? Usefulness, maybe. I felt useful. Delores Bernstein would be glad I'd solved the case. I couldn't be sure it would make her feel much better to know why her husband was killed, but at least she'd have a reason, and I hoped it would bring some closure. I knew something about the need for that.

"Not bad," Beach said. "What else do we need to do before I call an ambulance and bring in the real deputies to mop this place up?"

"Sam's down at Bobby G's house in Scottsdale. She tailed him home from Cactus Joe's after I talked to you earlier. I wanted to make sure we didn't lose track of him tonight. If Earl here wakes up, I think you'll be able to get him to finger Bobby G for the theft. I've got a nice confession to that effect on my iPhone if you need it. But I'd rather you guys get your own confession."

"Something wrong with yours?"

I didn't answer that. The confessions of Earl Johnson were obtained in a manner perhaps inconsistent with posse protocols. There were some things even my best friend didn't need to know. "Best if you get your own."

Beach looked at me long. Pursed his lips and nodded. "We'll get somebody to pick Bobby G up right away. You think he pulled the trigger?"

"Probably not. He'd have used Yuri Boiko for that. I'm guessing you'll find the handgun at Boiko's place. Boiko's not the smartest shooter around."

"You got that on your iPhone, too?"

"What do I look like, an amateur?"

Beach laughed out loud. Earl Johnson stirred.

"We'll work with the Scottsdale police to find Boiko," Beach said, "grab him soon as we can."

CHAPTER 23

We pulled up to the gate in the Jeep on a bright and cool Monday afternoon. SUVs were streaming into country club, bringing kids home from school. The temperature had dropped to around fifty overnight, cool for late April. The weather had shifted, and a few clouds billowed overhead. It was seventy-eight now, said the deejay on KJZZ. The deejay gave an audible shiver when he said it. It was the Valley of the Sun's version of spring volatility. It was glorious, and it would last only a day. Tomorrow's high, the deejay predicted: low nineties again.

Mike Martinson came out of the guard shack. "Hey, Mr. Quinn."

"Hi Mike. This is Sam Marcos. She's been helping me on the murder case."

Martinson looked around uncomfortably, not sure if he should say anything.

"It's all right. Sam knows what you did for me. It'll stay between us three."

He nodded. "How's it going, then?"

"Heading up to tell Delores Bernstein that we've solved the case. The bad guys have all been caught."

"What about Earl?"

"Interestingly, he's not behind bars."

Martinson frowned. His stoop seemed to increase.

"For some reason, he had to make a stop at the hospital first. Something about running into a door, then a hard fall, couple things broken. I'm not sure what happened."

"I see." Martinson pulled himself up to full height, smiled more than normal, revealing even more of his large teeth. "You wouldn't have had anything to do with that, I don't suppose."

"If I did, I wouldn't admit it. But let's keep that just between us, OK?"

Martinson nodded, then opened the gate and saluted us as we drove through.

***

Delores Bernstein brought coffee in, white cups on the tray. All three of us had some. Her eyes were red from crying.

"I'm so sorry, Delores," Sam said. "Is there anything we can do?"

"I've been crying ever since you phoned to tell me it looked like the murderer had been caught." She sniffed, then took a deep breath, closed her eyes. "Part of it was relief, an unexpected odd sense of joy that the murderers had been caught." She opened her eyes and gave Sam a serious stare. "Is that twisted?"

"Not at all," Sam said. "You needed to know what happened. With that knowledge came some relief. Joy doesn't seem a stretch from that."

"Thank you," Delores said. "Whether that's true or not, it feels good to hear you say it." She looked at me. "A lot of the tears today were just the ones I've been holding in while you looked into all this. Please tell me everything."

I went through the whole investigation, start to finish.

Delores didn't show any reaction. Just listened. When I was done, she asked: "Will they all go to jail?"

"The evidence is strong. I just heard before we drove up here that they ran the tests on the gun they found at Yuri Boiko's place. It's a match with the bullet they dug out of the garage floor."

Delores blinked. I lowered my eyes, wished I'd delivered that differently.

"And Earl Johnson confessed this morning," I added.

"Why did he confess?"

"Let's just say his arm was twisted a little," I said. "And there will be a deal made. The sheriff expects he'll testify against Bobby and Boiko, in exchange for a lighter sentence."

Delores thought about that a moment. She nodded once to indicate she was OK with such a deal.

"And the Franklin bust?" she asked.

"I wanted to talk to you about that," I said. "It's evidence, but I spoke with Jack Beachum on the posse and he says neither the sheriff nor the prosecutor want to hang onto a three million dollar piece of evidence for too long. They've photographed it and taken fingerprints, and they'd like to return it to you as soon as possible. You said you were never a big fan of sculpture. I know it might be hard, but I wondered if you'd be willing to part with it. The arrests will be on the six o'clock news tonight, Sam's colleague at The Republic is writing about it as we speak for the paper. The trial will probably be all over the media, and …"

"I don't want it here," she said. "At best, it'd be risking another break-in. At worst, it will be a constant reminder of Tinker's murder."

"If you like, we can call Sally McKann at the Franklin Institute. I think she'd be very interested to offer a fair price in exchange for not having to compete at auction. You might not get the best price, but the bust would be in good hands, and finally everyone would have an opportunity to enjoy it."

"Please do," Delores said.

"It's late evening in Philly," Sam said. "She probably won't be in."

"I have her cell."

Sam raised an eyebrow.

I dialed the number.

"Hi Sally. Eli Quinn."

"Mr. Quinn. I didn't expect to hear back from you so soon."

"We found the Franklin bust."

"That was fast," she said. "Usually stolen art isn't recovered at all. You must be a helluva detective."

"Or a very lucky one. Either way, I'm one-for-one."

"Your first case?"

"Yep."

"Impressive," she said. "So where is the bust now?"

"The sheriff has it, but to him it's a hot potato. Delores Bernstein, the wife of the man who bought the bust at auction, would like to see if you could offer a fair price for it, avoid the hassle of another auction, the chance of it eventually getting stolen a third time."

"That would be favorable," Sally McKann said. "I'll run it by the Board of Directors in the morning and give you a call. I think they'll be keen to add this to our collection, and I know we have the funds."

I clicked off. "I think you'll have a buyer by morning," I told Delores.

I suddenly felt exhausted. Four days of investigating, a couple of fights—quick and not too challenging, but both with my life on the line, not just points in a match—the tension of watching my back, worrying about Delores and Sam. "We should go," I said.

We went to the door. Delores reached into her purse and pulled out a crisp dollar bill. She handed it to me. I smiled and bowed slightly as I took it.

"Thank you, Mr. Quinn," she said. "Thank you."

CHAPTER 24

The flames of the fire stood straight up, licking the windless night. A dog barked somewhere far off, then it was quiet again.

We sat in the backyard on the iron chairs Jess had picked out, feet up on the fire pit. Solo rested his head on the chair arm, getting a well deserved rubbing all over his head and behind his ears. I inhaled the night, let the exhaustion settle into the chair. Images of Jess flicked through my mind the way they often did whenever I wasn't thinking on something else. I'd thought about her a little bit less the past four days. It didn't feel great to think about her less, but it felt necessary. I needed the memory to fade a bit, like an old photograph, so that I could cherish it rather than be absorbed by it. I didn't want to let the memory go. Knew I never would. Also knew I had to allow my life to move forward. It would happen in steps, many steps, and for the first time in nearly a year, I knew I'd taken a couple.

Through the patio speakers came the southwest-sounding guitar work from the movie *August Rush*, on a Pandora station started with *Zapata's Boots* by Tommy Guerrero. The song relied a little too much on harmonics for my taste, but it was nonetheless music that could sit in the background, not demanding to be listened to. Solo had wandered over to the edge of the flagstone, a corner he favored. He lay prone, a nylon bone between his crossed front paws, gnawing.

"You miss Jess," she said.

I took a moment to reply. "I do." I wondered how she knew what I was thinking.

"You always will."

"I know."

"If you've a date in Constantinople..."

"... she'll be waiting in Istanbul," I said.

"Maybe she will be."

"It's just a song."

"And a *Jeopardy* question."

"Yeah, easy one."

We didn't talk for a few minutes. We watched the fire. It changed every second, the gas-powered flames moving around, emanating from different places in the lava rocks. Steady but random, minds of their own.

"Delores told me she's going to donate the money from the bust," Sam said.

"She's a good woman. I wonder what she'll do with the insurance money."

"Going to donate that, too. She said she doesn't need the money. She's looking for suggestions. Wants it to go to something that benefits everyone in Pleasant."

I smiled in the darkness. Much good was coming from the solving of a crime. "I like it when the rich don't just get richer," I said. "She's a *really* good woman."

"Glass of wine?" Sam asked. "Beer?"

"Not tonight," I said. "I've been drinking too much lately. For a year, actually. Ever since ..."

"It's OK, Quinn. You don't have a drinking problem."

"I wonder sometimes."

"Do you want a drink tonight?"

"I do."

"It won't hurt to have one."

"I'm not worried about the first one."

We watched the fire. The quiet stayed quiet. Sam spoke again, almost a whisper.

"Your first case. You solved it pretty damn quick. You don't seem too happy about it."

"Not unhappy," I said. "Tired."

"Bother you what you did to Earl Johnson?"

"He got what he had coming. And he'll be fine, at least physically."

"You got a confession out of him, got him to finger his accomplices. The cops might not have gotten that on their own."

I nodded. We were both looking at the fire so she probably didn't see the nod.

"But you hurt him more than you had to."

"That's one way to look at it. There was a gun. We scuffled. My instincts took over. I don't feel bad about what I did."

We sat. Sam settled into her chair a bit, extended her arms on the iron chair arms.

"I'd have done the same to him," she said. "Maybe worse, if I were capable. Not sure I wouldn't kill somebody like that, end it there."

"Wouldn't be right to kill him. Just the force necessary to disarm and subdue."

"Plus maybe a little more."

"Maybe a little more."

"You're a complex man, Eli Quinn."

"You too," I said.

We fell into silence again. It was comfortable. More comfortable than ever.

ABOUT THE AUTHOR

Robert Roy Britt is the author of *Closure* and *Drone*, the first two books in the Eli Quinn detective series, and is at work on the third one. He lives in Arizona with his wife, their youngest son and two dogs. You can visit his website at robertroybritt.com.

If you liked this book, please review it on Amazon, Goodreads or wherever you get bookish. Reviews help sell books and allow Eli Quinn to take on more cases.

ACKNOWLEDGEMENTS

It took years to muster the time, energy and creativity to write this book. I'm grateful to my family for their encouragement and support. To Allison Wolcott, who believed in me for all those years and offered tremendous perspective that helped shape this book. To R.G., whose incredibly kind and helpful rejection letter seventeen years ago lit a fire. And to my sharp-eyed editor, Lauren Craft, who saves me from extreme embarrassment.

54001448R00089

Made in the USA
Lexington, KY
30 July 2016